HEART TRICK

KRISTEN GRANATA

D1519948

To all the girlies in their hockey romance era.

CASSIDY

THEN HE PENETRATES me with his cock.

"No, that doesn't sound right." I hold down the delete key with my index finger and start again.

He positions his tip at my entrance and slides inside.

"Entrance? What is her vagina, a portal?"

Delete.

He thrusts his shaft inside me and we cry out in pleasure as we embark on a journey of pure ecstasy.

"Jesus Christ, this is getting worse by the second." I slam my laptop shut and glare at my bird. "This is hopeless. I'm a lost cause."

Candy cocks her head.

"I'm really not in the mood for your positivity right now, okay? I'm wallowing. Let me wallow."

She hops onto the bottom perch in her cage and pecks at her food, letting me go on my self-pity spiral.

"Not only did Sheldon break my heart, but he took my writing mojo with him." I stab the air with my finger. "He's off living his life, having tons of hot cheater sex. Meanwhile, I'm sitting over here and I haven't so much as felt the touch of another man, let alone write about a fictional one. What kind of romance author has no romance in her life?" I let out a humorless laugh and shake my head. "A pathetic one, that's who."

Candy tweets like she agrees.

"I should be writing the best book of my life, and get revenge on my adulterous ex-boyfriend. He should be seeing my face on all the billboards in this city and have to deal with the fact that he lost me because he's the one who screwed it all up. And that would happen if I could just finish a damn book."

It's been a year-and-a-half since my last book release. It's not for lack of ideas. I have dozens of half-baked concepts saved on my MacBook. But whenever I get to a sex scene, I freeze up. Who knew getting cheated on would be a perpetual boner-killer?

"No, you know what? Fuck this, and fuck him. I'm going to finish this book if it kills me."

I open my laptop and try to start again, but voices in the hallway pull my attention.

I gasp. "It's my new neighbor!"

I fly off my chair and bolt to the door, stretching on my tippy-toes to reach the peephole.

A large man stands beside Rupert, the bellhop in our building. I smush my face against the door, straining to see what he looks like through the tiny fishbowl lens.

"He's very tall," I whisper-yell to Candy. "He has dark hair."

She chirps.

"I don't know. I can't tell if he's cute. He's facing away from me."

The man speaks to Rupert, revealing a deep voice. "Thanks. I can take it from here."

"Welcome to the building, sir. If you need anything at all, please let me know. My name is Rupert." Rupert shakes his hand and then stuffs his hand into his pocket after he pulls back. "Thank you very much, sir. That's very generous of you."

Neighbor Man tipped him. That's promising. Points for him.

After Rupert leaves, the man wheels the luggage cart inside his apartment.

My shoulders jump as his door slams shut behind him. I won't count that against him though. These doors are heavy and take some getting used to.

"I miss Sherry." I turn around and walk back to my desk wearing a frown. "I hope she's doing all right."

The elderly woman who lived next door to me for the last five years was recently moved to a nursing home. Her memory was on the decline and I know it was the right thing for her family to do, but I can't help feeling sad about it.

I slump down in my chair and run my fingertips over the keyboard, willing the words to flow. "All right. You're a small-town girl who just inherited her wealthy grandfather's estate in the big city. You move up there to go through his belongings, and you meet the handsome billionaire who's running his company. He sweeps you off your feet and you fall in love. Now it's time to bone him, goddamnit!"

I stare at the blinking cursor for the next twenty minutes. Not a single word comes out.

Maybe I'm just not feeling a spark between these characters. The reviews from my last book bounce off the walls of my brain like a pinball.

One star: A lackluster plot with two-dimensional characters.

Two stars: This didn't feel like Quinn's previous work.

One star: DNFed this at twenty percent.

One star: The characters had no chemistry.

I can't blame the readers. I know it wasn't my best work. My relationship was on the rocks and I wasn't into the story. But it kills me that my readers could tell that from my writing.

My phone vibrates on the desk, pulling me from my intrusive thoughts.

I swipe my thumb across the screen. "Hey, Aarya."

"Hey, boo. What are you doing?"

I heave an overdramatic sigh. "Oh, you know, just sitting here writing the worst book in the history of mankind—no, wait. Scratch that. To write the worst book, that would mean I'd have to actually be writing."

"Still no luck with the book, huh?"

"Nope. My creativity has dried up like an old sponge."

"It'll come back to you."

"What if it doesn't? What if the last book I published is it for me?"

"It's not. You're just in a slump. Sometimes you're up, and sometimes you're down. It happens to the best of us artists."

I run my fingers through my hair and pull at the roots. "How are you? What are you up to today?"

"I just left the gallery. I want to get a workout in before dinner tonight. You feel like meeting me at the gym?"

"Hell yes. I need to blow off some steam." I close my laptop and head to my bedroom. "I'll meet you down there in ten."

"Sounds good. Oh, and please don't take that pre-workout again. You were like a feral squirrel last time."

I scoff as I pull out a sports bra from my dresser drawer. "I was not."

"You looked like you were on speed and washed it down with a Red Bull. Dump that shit in the garbage."

"I don't like your tone today."

She laughs. "When do you ever?"

Several minutes later, I meet Aarya at the gym in our apartment building. We head to the ellipticals first.

"I'm assuming you didn't write anything today?"

I pull my hair into a ponytail as I start pumping my legs. "I can't get out of my own head. Every time I try to write, it's like I'm staring at this blank wall and I can't figure out how to get around it."

"Every author experiences writer's block once in a while. Maybe you're trying too hard. You can't force it."

"But the more I avoid it, the longer it's going to be until I can finish the book."

"Or the longer you obsess over it, the harder it's going to be to achieve. Take a break from it. Do something else. Get a hobby. You spend too much time with that serial killer bird of yours."

My eyebrows press together as I toss a glare her way. "She only killed one bird. She's not a serial killer."

"Fine. She's a plain old murderer then." Aarya scrunches her nose. "I don't know how you sleep with that thing in your home after what she did."

Five years ago, I found a fallen bird's nest out on the sundeck with two baby Cardinals in it. The mother was nowhere in sight and they looked hurt, so I nursed them back to health. But after doing some research, I learned that the mother wouldn't come back to take care of them if she smelled a human on them. Rather than send them back into the wild to fend for themselves and likely die, I bought a cage and named them Maggie and Wally. Everything was great until I came home one night and found Wally dead on the bottom of their cage. Maggie pecked him to death and sat there on her swing with his feathers sticking out of her bloody beak as if everything was fine.

I'll never know what the real reason for the murder was, but Maggie was pissed off about something and I can't blame her for that. Female Cardinals aren't as vibrant in color as the stunning bright-red males, so maybe she was jealous of her beautiful brother. Maybe he just shit in her birdseed. Regardless, I bought her a new cage and changed her name to Candy—after Candice Montgomery, the woman who axed her friend to death forty-one times and walked free.

I thought it was fitting.

"I love Candy despite what she did, like a good mother should. Plus, she's an excellent listener and—oh, look!" I hunch down and lower my voice. "There's my new neighbor."

The tall, dark-haired man stands with his back to us as he fills out paperwork at the front desk.

"Did you meet him already?" Aarya asks.

"No. I saw him through my peephole when Rupert moved him in. Couldn't see his face though."

Her eyes narrow as she strains to see him across the gym. "He's certainly a big boy."

Gray joggers hug his tree-trunk thighs and ass. His white T-shirt stretches from shoulder to shoulder across his broad back.

Come on, Neighbor Man. Turn around. Let's see what you look like.

He takes what feels like forever filling out his gym membership forms, but then he turns and enters the cardio area.

"Damn," Aarya murmurs.

Damn is right. Neighbor Man has a thick jaw covered in dark scruff. His messy hair falls in his eyes and curls around his ears. His nose has a slight bend in it, like it was broken at some point. He's the walking definition of rugged. Between his size and his hardened expression, he looks menacing.

"How old do you think he is?" I whisper.

"Mid-to-late thirties maybe."

I nod in agreement. He definitely looks older than me.

He skips cardio and heads straight for the squat rack, which is conveniently located directly in front of the row of ellipticals.

Aarya waggles her eyebrows. "Showtime, baby."

I roll my lips together and avert my eyes. "He's in front of the mirror. He can see you ogling him."

"Don't act like you don't want to watch him drop that ass right now."

I do. I really do.

"Fine. I'm going to watch one squat and then I'm going to work out."

Once Neighbor Man racks the plates on either side of the metal bar, he ducks under it and positions it on his traps, squaring his feet hip-width apart. I hold my breath as he squats down and presses back up.

Aarya hisses. "I'd let him bend down over my face like that and put his balls right in my mouth if he wanted to."

A loud laugh bursts from my throat, garnering the attention of several people nearby, including my neighbor. "Okay, that's it. I'm going to finish my workout far, far away from you."

Aarya keeps her eyes zeroed on his ass like a laser. "I'll be right here."

I shake my head and make my way to the dumbbells.

And I only check out my hot neighbor twice in the reflection of the mirror.

After I finish my usual routine for bis and tris, I say goodbye to

Aarya as she heads for the sauna. I step inside the elevator, press the button for the sixth floor, and dab my forehead with my towel as the door slides closed.

Then a giant hand shoots out and the door slides open again.

Neighbor Man steps inside.

I smile up at him as I press my back against the cool metal wall to give him space, though he doesn't smile back because he doesn't even look at me.

He glances at the illuminated six on the panel before leaning against the opposing wall without a word, staring straight ahead at nothing.

Everyone in the building gives a courteous *hello* when they share an elevator. It's elevator etiquette. Common decency.

I suppress a groan. *Please don't be a dick.* Sherry was so sweet. She gave the best hugs, and even better advice. We spent every Tuesday and Thursday night together playing Rummy. I cooked and she baked. She was the greatest neighbor a girl could ask for.

Sadness sits on my chest like a weighted blanket.

I miss you, Sher.

After a loud ding, the door slides open. Neighbor Man doesn't move, allowing me to step into the hallway ahead of him.

So, he won't say hello but he displays a modicum of courtesy by letting the woman step out first.

Interesting.

I can feel his presence behind me as we walk. He could easily pass me to get to his door, but he takes his time at a slow pace.

I reach my door and pretend to fumble with my purse as I get out my key card, allowing him enough time to get to his door on my left.

I glance over at him and act like I haven't realized he's been in the hallway with me this whole time. "Oh, hey. You're my new neighbor."

His dark eyes meet mine for a brief moment. "Looks that way."

Before I can stick out my hand and introduce myself, he swings open his door and steps inside his apartment, letting the door slam shut behind him.

Okay now that *slam was on purpose.*

2

TRENTON

I ROLL onto my stomach and slam the pillow over my head in an attempt to drown out the shrill noise floating through the wall.

Maybe I'll suffocate myself under here and I won't have to be subjected to my neighbor's off-key singing ever again.

I used to love the song *Africa*. Now, I'll cringe every time I hear it on the radio. The woman next door just ruined Toto for me along with my morning.

Since there's no way I can fall back asleep now, I fling off the covers and stalk into the bathroom to take a piss and brush my teeth.

My annoying neighbor is just the icing on the cake that is my new life.

Last year, my fiancé cheated on me. I could've dealt with that—honestly, I could've moved on. I had a great hockey career, and a team I loved being a part of. But she had to go and cheat on me with my teammate. It caused such a rift in the team that the General Manager traded me after the season ended. He might as well have put me out to pasture, because that's what it feels like. I'm the thirty-six-year-old on a new team, which doesn't bode well. They'll be pushing me to retire in no time. This is the beginning of the end for me.

And then what? What will I have without hockey?

I brush my gums so vigorously, I'm surprised I don't spit blood when I rinse out my mouth. I woke up feeling angry today, and it's more than the fact that my sleep was interrupted by a screeching serenade. I'm angry about looking like a fool. About losing my teammates. About the way this whole thing went down. Kicked off *my* team. Forced to move out of *my* city.

I'm the one who got cheated on, so why am I paying for their indiscretion?

The worst part of it all? I went quietly. The news exploded all over the country and everyone's talking about the scandal. Yet I kept my mouth shut and left without a fight.

But the shock and denial have worn off. I'm in my anger phase now. The gym is one of the only places I can unleash it, so I change into my gym clothes and grab my duffle bag on the way out of my apartment.

I'm so absorbed in my own thoughts that I don't realize the singing bandit next door is exiting her apartment at the same time. She smacks into me and I almost barrel right through her. I catch her before she hits the ground, gripping her shoulders as I steady her.

She smooths down her hair as she blinks up at me. "Geez. Where's the fire?"

"Sorry. I didn't see you."

"Of course you didn't."

My chin jerks back. "What's that supposed to mean?"

She mutters something under her breath before she spins around and heads down the hallway. Judging by the spandex clinging to her body, she's headed to the same place I am.

Great.

We wait for an elevator, and when one opens up, she steps inside and presses the button for the gym level.

"Where are you going?" she asks.

I gesture to the illuminated G on the panel.

She nods and leans her hip against the wall as we descend.

She's hot. It's hard not to notice. Thick and curvy with long brown hair. Admittedly, I watched her ass sway in front of me as she walked to her apartment door yesterday. I figure it was only fair since she and her friend were staring at *my* ass during my workout like I was on stage at a Magic Mike show.

I should be used to it after a decade of being in the spotlight, but everything has been different once the news about my fiancé cheating on me with my best friend got out. It's like an alert was sent out to single women everywhere: "Heartbroken Hockey Player Needs Healing." Puck bunnies have been throwing themselves at me worse than before.

So, when this woman smiled at me in the elevator yesterday, I counted the seconds until she asked if I was the person she thought I was. That's always how it starts. "You look familiar," or, "Are you Trent Ward?" Some women are bold enough to slip me their numbers and tell me how they can help me get over my ex—which is why I try to ignore everyone I can.

Today though, she doesn't smile at me. Maybe it's because I bulldozed her upstairs, or maybe she's just in a shit mood and it has nothing to do with me. But when the elevator door opens, she bolts like she can't get away from me fast enough.

She heads to the left and I make my way to the squat rack. I set down my water bottle and lift the bar to do a warmup set of bicep curls before adding any weight. Halfway through my set, my neighbor appears at my side holding a twenty-five-pound plate in each hand—glaring at me in the reflection of the mirror.

"Excuse me. I was going to use the squat rack."

Is she for real?

I arch a brow as I continue my set. "I didn't see anyone standing here when I got here."

"I went to get plates." She holds them up as if I don't see them.

"Well, it'll be all yours when I'm done."

Her cheeks redden. "It's Gym Etiquette 101: Don't use the free-standing squat rack for anything other than squats. You can do your bicep curls literally anywhere else."

I've lost count of how many reps I've done, but I won't stop now.

"Pretend I'm doing squats, and go do something else while you wait your turn."

She grits her teeth as she storms away.

Who the hell does she think she is ordering me around? Are these the kind of self-righteous rich people who live in this building?

I'd be lying if I said I didn't drag out my set a bit longer than necessary just to spite her.

When I finish, I spot her by the cables. She has the strap wrapped around her ankle as she swings her leg out to the side. Now, I *could* steer clear of her and go about the rest of my workout. I should. But something about her attitude today has me heading straight for her. It's like I have an itch that needs scratching.

"They have machines for that, you know," I say.

She glances over her shoulder and her eyes narrow on me. Then she lifts her chin and continues swinging her leg out to the side.

"I don't need workout tips. I know what I'm doing."

I fold my arms over my chest. "But you're using the cables for people who are trying to do upper body."

"Much like the dumbbells can be used for biceps, yet there you were, curling in the squat rack."

"So, it's okay only when you do it? That's pretty hypocritical of you."

She rolls her eyes. "This is totally not the same thing."

I'm about to fire back but she swings her leg extra wide, her foot coming so close to my balls that I have to step out of the way.

She gives me a phony-ass sweet smile. "It'll be all yours when I'm done. Now wait your turn like a good boy."

Tell me why my dick twitches when she says that?

A frustrated growl bubbles up in my throat, but I say nothing as I walk away. If she wants a reaction out of me, she won't get one.

Not even when she follows me to the elevator at the end of my workout and gets in beside me. We stand on our respective sides until the door opens and then walk down the hall in silence.

But when we get to our apartment doors, she speaks. "Since you're unaware of gym etiquette, let me give you another friendly piece of advice about being a good neighbor: If you hold onto your doorknob, the door won't slam so loud."

I turn my head to meet her pointed stare. "What?"

"You slam your door every time you walk in and out. It's a little jarring."

Now she's just fucking with me. She has to be. I've only been here for two days. How many times could I have slammed my door?

I prop my door open with my foot. "Speaking of jarring noises, I did hear something this morning. Does this building have a cat problem?"

Her eyes narrow. "A cat problem?"

"This morning I was woken up to the sound of what I assumed was a dying cat. But I suppose a cat wouldn't know all the words to a Toto song, so maybe I'm wrong."

Her cheeks turn a deep shade of red as she plants her hand on her hips. "I've never had any complaints before you got here."

"Maybe your last neighbor was hard of hearing."

She scoffs. "Well, she certainly didn't slam the door so hard that my entire apartment rattled."

This is ridiculous. How can one stranger have this kind of effect on me? I don't act like this to people, especially those I don't know. My PR agent would chew my ass out if she could see me. I'm supposed to keep my head down and stay out of the public eye, not draw more attention to myself. For all I know, this crazy woman could be recording me as we speak, and tomorrow I'll be all over the news cycle again.

Instead of continuing this any further, I end it by walking inside my apartment.

And I may or may not let the door slam behind me on purpose.

"Do you have any questions?"

My eyes bounce around the locker room. "Do you have cold tubs?"

Coach nods. "We just had our facility renovated, and we offer hot and cold tubs in the training facility."

"We upgraded just in time for you, Warden." A man with coppery curls walks out of the shower area with a towel wrapped low around his waist. "Coach heard what a sweet facility you had in Seattle so he made sure to trick this place out."

"Not true." Coach heaves a sigh. "Trenton Ward, this is Stephen McKinley."

I reach out to shake his hand, but he pulls me in for a hug. His towel slips and he makes no effort to reach for it. Coach snatches the towel off the floor and tosses it at him.

McKinley wraps the towel around the back of his neck. "Glad to have you on our team, man."

"Jesus, Mac. Don't scare off our new goalie with your giant monster dick between your legs." Another man emerges from the shower, his towel tightly tucked around his waist.

McKinley grins. "Hey, I just wanted to show him that the carpet matches the drapes. People wonder about that."

"Literally no one wonders about that." He shakes my hand like a normal person. "Jason Stamos. Nice to meet you."

I studied the players before arriving in Jersey City. Stephen "Mac" McKinley is a left wing forward, and Jason "Stams" Stamos is on defense. The team has an impressive starting lineup, and this season looks promising for them.

For me as well now, I guess.

McKinley cups his hands over his mouth. "Hey, Krum Cake. Stop jerking off in the shower and get out here so you can meet our new goalie."

Stamos chuckles. "Don't piss him off, Mac. He's in a shit mood today."

"When is he not in a shit mood?"

Coach pinches the bridge of his nose. "Well, I'll leave you to get acquainted with the boys. If you have any questions, don't hesitate to come see me."

"Thanks, Coach."

He clasps my hand. "We're happy to have you on the team."

I nod. "Happy to be here."

After Coach exits the locker room, a tall bearded man steps out of the shower and glares at McKinley.

Alexander Krumkachova. Team Captain and center. One of the best players currently in the NHL.

"Welcome to the team." He shakes my hand. "Sorry about what happened to you. That's some bush league shit if you ask me."

Good, let's address the elephant in the room and get it over with.

I hike a nonchalant shoulder as if being betrayed and then traded hasn't crippled me. "It is what it is."

Krumkachova shakes his head. "You don't have to worry about shit like that here. You're a Goldfinch now, and we're family."

I thought my last team was my family.

Look how that turned out.

"All I want is to play hockey," I say.

"And hockey you shall play." McKinley slaps his palms together. "It's going to be a great season, boys. I can smell it."

It will be a great season, and I'll make sure of it.

I have everything to prove, and nothing left to lose.

3

CASSIDY

My alarm goes off at 5:00AM.

Showtime.

I turn on my Bluetooth speaker and crank up the volume as high as I can. This morning's performance is brought to you by Heart. No one can belt out the high notes like Ann Wilson, but when I sing *Alone* in the shower, I sure as shit try to.

A smile stretches across my face as I head to the bathroom. If Neighbor Man can hear me singing through the wall, then our layouts mirror each other, making his bathroom and bedroom right on the other side of mine. I take a long, hot shower, really letting the steam warm up my vocal cords. One song turns into five, and after my concert, I feel satisfied and ready to tackle my day.

That asshole won't sleep in another day in his life if I have anything to say about it.

Who does he think he is, slamming doors and using up gym equipment with that smug attitude?

"Good morning, Candy." I pop open the door to her cage. "How did you sleep?"

She hops across her perch and tilts her head.

"I'm going to have a breakthrough today. I'm going to write. I can feel it." I sit down in my plush yellow chair, and open my laptop. "I'm going to write, and nothing is going to stop me."

I square my shoulders and wait for the words to come to me.

Five minutes pass and then I reach for my phone. "I need to be inspired. Universe, send me something inspiring."

I click on the TikTok icon, hoping to come across something that will spark my creativity.

"Hockey." Swipe. "Hockey." Swipe. "More hockey."

I let out a loud groan. Readers are in their hockey romance era right now and I can't for the life of me figure out why. Sports are *so* boring. Men put these athletes up on a pedestal. Society pays them as if they've found the cure for cancer. And for what? Because they're athletic? Who cares if Michael Jordan can slam dunk a field goal or whatever it is he does?

A notification pops up on my screen.

BookishBrittney: When is your next release coming out? I've read all your books and I'm impatiently waiting for more!

I CLICK on her comment to respond to her video and prop up my phone on my desk before hitting record.

"I know, I know. It has been a while since I've published a book, but I can promise you I'm hard at work trying to finish this next one. I've been having a bit of writer's block lately and..."

I stop the video and delete the clips. I don't want anyone to know how much I've been struggling to write. It'll only fuel the trolls who keep telling me that my career is over because my last book sucked. It's why I haven't been posting on social media as much.

Bang!

My shoulders jerk up to my ears with the slam of my neighbor's door. I whip around and glare at the wall as if laser beams will shoot out of my eyeballs and sear into him when he walks by.

Then I get an idea.

I clear my throat and restart the video.

"My new neighbor is an asshole. Mind you, he just moved in a few days ago, but things have escalated rather quickly. I'm sitting here, minding my own business writing my next book, and every time he walks in or out of his apartment, he slams the door. And sure, the doors are heavy. One could argue that maybe he had something in his hands and didn't catch the door in time. Fine. But it has happened more than once, and it's the equivalent of a small-scale earthquake when this man is around.

"Now, I'm a nice neighbor. I don't want to start trouble. So, I ignored the slamming, and tried to smile and say hello. We were sharing an elevator, and I know he saw me, but he stepped inside and completely ignored me as if I didn't exist. Strike two for Neighbor Man. But I told myself, self, maybe he's oblivious and has so much going on inside his own head that he doesn't notice people around him. Until yesterday."

I take a dramatic pause before retelling the events from the gym yesterday, explaining to my followers who aren't familiar with the gym that one does not do bicep curls in the squat rack unless they want to be shunned by the gym community.

"By the end of my workout, I was pissed, and when we got to our doors, something inside me snapped. I decided to offer him a helpful tidbit of neighborly advice about how not to slam his door. Well, Neighbor Man proceeded to tell me that he could hear me singing through the walls and called me a shitty singer—which I am not, by the way. My mother used to call me her little songbird when I was little. So, I know he was just trying to get under my skin. And as if that wasn't bad enough, he slams his door in my face. Again!"

I continue recording and laugh while I tell my followers how I've decided to retaliate with early-morning singing. It's petty and imma-ture, I know, but I am so done with entitled assholes like him thinking they can do whatever they want to the people around them.

After I edit the clips, I click post.

Candy chirps and gives me what I interpret as a discerning look.

"Don't judge me, girl. You murdered your own brother. I don't want to hear it."

An hour later, I still haven't typed more than ten words, which I end up deleting because they're the worst ten words in the history of words.

My phone buzzes with an incoming FaceTime from Aarya.

"Hey, girl."

"Oh my god. Your TikTok video is going viral right now."

My eyebrows pinch together. "Which one?"

"The one you just posted, like, an hour ago. It already has over 50,000 views."

"The one about Neighbor Man?" I open the app to see what she's talking about. "Holy shit, you're right."

"This is genius marketing. People are going to see that you're an author and then they'll want to check out your books."

"This wasn't a marketing tactic. I was just pissed when I posted it."

"It doesn't matter now. You have to keep posting. People want updates."

I scroll through the comments and a loud laugh rips from my throat. "They think this is the premise to my next book."

"That's actually not a bad idea."

I let out a sardonic laugh. "Yeah, right. And I'd call it, *Enemies Minus the Lovers*."

"I'm serious. If you're stuck on the current book you're writing, then try something new. Plus, you'll have lots to write about because it's all true stuff that happened. It writes itself."

I chew on my bottom lip.

She's not wrong.

"Let's meet up for drinks and we can start outlining the book."

My eyebrows jump. "You want to plot it out with me?"

"Only because it's about your hot new neighbor."

I roll my eyes. "He's not hot. He's an asshole."

She shoots me a dubious look.

"Okay, fine. He's both."

"How many times has he called you?"

I click ignore and turn my phone face-down on the table. "Third time today."

Aarya sips her Cosmo. "Aren't you the least bit curious why your ex is calling you out of the blue?"

"Nope. I have nothing to say to him. I could never speak to him again for the rest of my life and I'd be perfectly okay with that. Actually, you know what?" I pick up my phone again and click on Sheldon's name before tapping *block caller*. "There. Done."

"Good for you."

"What could he possibly have to say? *I'm off having amazing sex with the woman I cheated on you with. How are you doing?*" I roll my eyes. "Spare me."

"I think it's time you get yourself back out there in the dating world. It's been well over a year. Why don't you sign up for Match.com or Hinge, or even Bumble?"

I scrunch my nose. "No thanks."

"Dude, I can literally hear your vagina crying."

I scoff. "She is well-taken care of, thank you very much."

"Your vibrator isn't enough, and you know it." Aarya sets down her martini glass and levels me with a look. "And it's not just sex. Just because Sheldon cheated on you doesn't mean you can't trust anyone else ever again."

"I'm not saying all men are lying, cheating, bags of dicks like Sheldon. But I'm just not into online dating." I gesture to Aarya. "Look at you. Look at all the crazy online dates you've been on. I don't want to go through that. I'd rather meet a guy the old-fashioned natural way."

"But you don't go anywhere, so how are you going to meet someone holed up in your apartment all the time?"

"I'm writing. That's what I need to focus on right now." I grimace. "Or at least I'm *trying* to write."

Her eyes light up. "Speaking of writing, let's discuss your new book about your hot neighbor."

I smirk. "I love how you're suddenly interested in my writing."

She feigns offense and places her palm on her chest. "Of course I'm interested in your writing."

"Name one book of mine that you've read."

"The one with the...the...uh, the guy with the thing, and they went on, like a boat or something?"

I tilt my head back as I laugh. "I've never written a book about a guy on a boat."

Aarya's shoulders droop. "Fine, I've never read your books, but that doesn't mean I'm a bad friend. I just hate reading. And romance books are so fake a corny. Real life doesn't happen like that."

I heave a sigh and prop my head up in my hand with my elbow on the table. "I know sometimes it feels that way, but true love is real."

She arches a sleek brow. "One person who's made for you and only you? No way."

"Maybe not one person, but a series of people you're destined to meet along the way."

"You're going to meet people whether you're destined to or not." She hikes a shoulder. "Plus, I like being single and fucking around. I don't need someone getting attached to me, and then I have to meet their parents who pressure you to get married and pop out babies."

"Love is different for everyone. You don't have to get married and have kids. You could have incredible sex and travel the world together."

She waves a dismissive hand. "I don't need romance to do that."

I smile. "You're going to meet someone one day, and he or she is going to knock you right on your ass. You'll see."

She points her index finger at me. "Don't you wish that monog-amous shit on me. Take it back!"

"Nope."

She flings a breadstick at me. "Take it back, bitch!"

The breadstick hits me in the shoulder and I laugh. "Fine, I take it back."

But I don't mean it. Love finds everyone, whether you're looking for it or not. And one day, my fiercely independent best friend is going to fall in love.

I just hope love is in the cards for me too.

4

CASSIDY

"Five-thousand words."

Aarya gasps. "Oh my god. That's a great start."

"I know." I kill the engine and lean back against the headrest. "It feels good to write again. This is what I've missed for so long."

"And all you needed was a little inspiration."

"Thanks for pushing me to write about Neighbor Man."

"Thank yourself for making that TikTok—which we need an update for, by the way."

My lips tug into a frown. "I haven't seen him in a couple of days."

"No more slamming door?"

"Nope. I didn't blast my music yesterday, and he didn't slam his door."

"Well, you need to have a run-in with him because you need more content."

I laugh. "You want me to stage a run-in?"

"Think of it as part of your job. You need him to continue writing your book."

I shake my head. "All right, let me go. I have to lug these groceries inside before my ice cream melts all over my back seat."

"Fine, but think about it."

"I will."

I forgot all my shopping totes at home—does anyone ever remember them? —so I refused to buy more than one at the grocery store out of pure spite. I managed to stuff all of my items into one bag. Now all I have to do is make it to the sixth floor.

I shut the door and click the alarm on my key fob, but gasp when I turn around.

No fucking way.

"Sheldon." I clutch at my chest. "Pro tip: Don't lurk in a parking garage if you're not trying to scare a woman."

"I'm sorry. I didn't mean to scare you." His eyes trail down the length of my body. "You look...you look great."

I position the ninety-pound grocery bag in front of me. "Why are you here?"

"I really hate the way we left things. I know we haven't spoken in a while but, I don't know. I just wanted to see you."

I blink once. Twice. Then a loud laugh rips from my throat. "Are you fucking serious right now?"

He grimaces. "I know, I know. I have a lot of nerve coming here like this, but—"

"But nothing. Where's Alicia? Shouldn't you be with her? Or are you cheating on her too?"

He steps forward and clasps my hand. "I broke up with her. I wasn't happy. It was fun in the beginning but it wore off."

I yank my hand out of his hold and step backward, my ass hitting my car. "Fun in the beginning—meaning when you were still with me."

He grimaces. "That came out wrong."

I roll my eyes. "I don't know why you thought you could come here."

"I miss you. I know I fucked up but I made a mistake and I was hoping you could give me a second chance."

My chin jerks back. "I want nothing to do with you, Sheldon. You had your chance with me and you blew it."

"I'm sorry, Cass." He steps into my space again. "I'm sorry I hurt you. I regret it every single day."

"Good. You should." I move around him and speed-walk across the parking lot.

He jogs after me. "Please, can we just talk?"

"No."

He reaches out and grabs my wrist. "Please, wait."

"I said no. Leave me alone, Sheldon." As I pull back my arm, the strap on the tote breaks, and all of my groceries go tumbling onto the ground.

"Hey!"

Both of our heads whip around at the sound of the bellowing voice.

Oh, for God's sake.

Neighbor Man stalks over to Sheldon and shoves his chest, sending him stumbling backward. "Keep your hands off of her."

Sheldon regains his footing and his hands shoot up on either side of his head. "I wasn't trying to hurt her."

He shoves Sheldon again. "Then why are her groceries all over the damn place, huh?"

"Tell him, Cass." Sheldon's Adam's apple bobs in his throat as he glances at me for help. "I just came here to talk."

Neighbor Man turns his head and looks at me over his shoulder, waiting for me to clarify.

I arch a brow and purse my lips. "I don't want to talk to you, Sheldon. Not now and not ever."

Sheldon's eyes narrow as they flick to my neighbor. "Is this your boyfriend?"

Sure, I could be honest and tell him no...but I guess I'm petty. "He is none of your business. Now go home and leave me alone."

Neighbor Man moves to stand beside me, but he angles himself so that he's half-blocking me from Sheldon.

"Wait a second." Sheldon tips his head like he recognizes Neighbor Man from somewhere. "Holy shit, are you—"

My neighbor lunges forward and grabs the collar of Sheldon's shirt, bringing his face close to his own. "I'll give you three seconds to get out of here before I remove you myself."

Damn. He's kind of hot when his temper isn't directed at me.

Sheldon scurries across the parking lot, and my neighbor stares after him until he disappears through the entrance of the garage. He's standing like a statue, muscles taut and hands balled into fists.

I clear my throat. "Thanks for that."

He turns his attention back to me, his eyes scanning my body. "Are you okay?"

I sweep my arm out and gesture to my groceries. "Just some bruised apples."

Neighbor Man kneels down and collects the items at our feet, stuffing them back inside the tote bag, while I chase after the runaway apples. One of them rolled underneath someone's car, so I flatten myself against the asphalt and stretch out my arm until my fingertips graze it.

I stand up and brush off the dirt from my tank top, and Neighbor Man takes the apples from me. He's holding the bag from the bottom, cradling it in his left arm.

I reach out for the bag. "Thank you. I can take it from here."

"I've got it. We're both going to the same place."

Oh.

I'm not going to argue with the guy after he just made Sheldon shit his pants and run away screaming like a little girl on a playground, so we head into the building and step into the elevator.

"That was my ex." I don't know why I feel the need to explain myself, but he's not speaking and I can't revert to awkward silence after what just happened downstairs.

"He seems like a real winner."

I let out a humorless laugh. "Yeah. He cheated on me and now he says he want me back."

Neighbor Man stares down at the bag in his arms.

"That was really kind of you to step in like you did," I continue.

He hikes a shoulder like it was no big deal. "You looked like you needed help."

"Well, it was nice of you to help me when you hate me."

His eyes dart to mine. "I don't hate you. I don't even know you."

I rack my brain for a quippy remark, but I come up empty. I should say something else. I'm a writer; you'd think I'd have an arsenal of dialogue at the ready. But what is there left to say? He helped me, and I've thanked him. Conversation over.

The elevator door opens and he gestures for me to walk ahead of him.

When we get to my door, I pull out my key card and open the door, propping it open with my foot as I take the bag from Neighbor Man.

He walks to his own door and unlocks it, but before he steps inside, he turns his head and meets my gaze. "I've been making an attempt to shut my door quieter."

I blink, unable to tell if he's making a joke or if he's waiting for me to concur with his statement.

"I haven't been killing any cats either."

"No, but there is a very vocal bird in that menagerie of yours."

I scowl, and the corner of his lips twitch. Then he closes his door—quietly—behind him.

I bolt inside and post the entire interaction on TikTok.

5

CASSIDY

"There's no way in hell that I'm going to this reunion. I mean, right? Why would I go? I hated high school. Plus, Sheldon will be there. I don't need him annoying me all night."

Candy pecks at her food dish.

"I'm a successful author though. I've done well for myself. It would be nice to rub it in everyone's faces. Isn't that what a high school reunion is really for?"

Candy chirps.

"Yeah, you're right. Fuck them all."

I toss the invitation on top of the pile of mail on my desk and kick off the floor to spin in my chair.

"It's going to be a great day today. I wrote so much last night and I think I even smoothed everything over with Neighbor Man. Oh, let's check the video I posted."

But when I unlock my phone, I see five missed calls from Aarya. My stomach drops. I click on her name and she answers on the first ring.

"Girl, where have you been? I've been calling you for the last hour."

"What's wrong? Are you okay?"

She coughs out an incredulous laugh. "Am I okay? Hmm, let's

28

see. My best friend is dating a famous hockey player and she didn't tell me. How do you think I'm doing right now?"

My eyebrows pinch together. "What? Who? I thought I was your best friend."

"I'm talking about you, numbnuts. How could you not tell me about Neighbor Man?"

My eyes dart around the room, not focusing on anything in particular as I try to piece together Aarya's frantic words. "I am so confused. What are you talking about?"

"Click on the link I texted you and see for yourself."

I pull the phone away from my ear and click on the link in her message. The page opens to a BuzzFeed article, but I couldn't tell you what the headline reads because right underneath the bold words is a picture of Neighbor Man.

And me.

In my parking garage.

"What the hell?" I scroll down to find more snapshots taken from the altercation with Sheldon last night. One shows my neighbor with Sheldon's shirt in his fists, and several others are of the two of us after Sheldon left.

"Aarya, who would've taken these pictures?"

"It looks like paparazzi."

"Since when do I have paparazzi?"

"Read the article, babe."

I scan the first paragraph and choke on my own spit. "Neighbor Man is in the NHL?"

"He's not just in the NHL. He's one of the best goalies of all-time. You didn't know?"

"No! How would I know? I don't even know his name, let alone his profession."

She pauses. "So, you're not secretly dating him and keeping it from me?"

"Of course not. This article is taken completely out of context." I continue scanning the page, and let out an incredulous laugh. "They referred to me as the *smut writer girlfriend*. That's all they can ever focus on—the fact that I write sex scenes in my books. What about character development? What about the rest of the whole damn storyline?"

"This is kind of cool."

I scoff. "Hardly."

"You were photographed by the paparazzi."

"Only by association. They were looking for Neighbor Man, not me. Besides, I don't—" Three hard knocks on my door stop me mid-sentence. "Shit. Someone's at my door."

I tiptoe across the room and peer into the peephole.

"It's Neighbor Man," I whisper.

"Open the door," Aarya whispers back. "He probably wants to talk about the article."

"Why are you whispering too?"

"I don't know."

"What do you think he wants?"

The deep voice on the other side of the door speaks. "I can hear you whispering, you know."

My cheeks burn. "I'll call you back, Aarya."

"You fucking better."

I end the call and swing open my door, and a tall red-headed woman pushes past me.

"Excuse me. Who are you?" My head whips to my neighbor. "Who is she?"

"The question is: Who are *you*?" The woman now standing in my living room smiles as she holds out her hand. "I'm Celeste. I'm Trent's PR agent."

I shake her hand because it's the polite thing to do, but I keep my gaze on my neighbor. "You have a PR agent?"

He heaves a sigh as he enters my apartment and locks the door behind him. "Have you seen the news at all today?"

"I know. It's terrible what happened to that little boy in Newark. I don't know how those parents are going to live with themselves after that. Hopefully they stop smoking."

The both of them blink at me like I'm an alien speaking Korean.

"Oh, you mean the article where the whole world thinks we're dating? Yeah, I saw that one."

Celeste barks out a laugh and Trenton pinches the bridge of his nose.

"I love you already." Celeste makes herself comfortable on my couch and pats the cushion beside her. "Let's chat about what we're going to do."

I lower myself beside her. "What is there to do exactly? It's a silly little article. We weren't doing anything scandalous. It'll blow over."

"Well, that's the thing." Celeste crosses her long legs. "We want to run with this story."

My chin jerks back and my eyes dart to Trenton, who's frozen by my door as if he's afraid to step one more foot inside my apartment.

"Would you come sit down so we can discuss this like grown adults?" Celeste waves him over.

Before he can answer, Candy flutters out of her cage and makes a beeline for Trenton's head. She gets curious whenever guests are over, and she likes to hover in front of their faces to check them out.

The two-hundred-and-something-pound man drops to the ground like he's under attack. "Jesus Christ, what is that thing?"

Celeste cackles. "Oh my god, it's a bird."

"Sorry about that." I jump up and lock the cage door once Candy is back inside. "She's just saying hello."

"She tried to take my eye out." He peeks over the back of the couch. "You let her fly around your apartment?"

I hike a shoulder and drop back down on the couch beside Celeste. "Why not?"

"Uh, because it could peck you to death? Or shit on the floor. Birds are dirty creatures."

I glance over my shoulder. "Don't listen to him, Candy. You're perfect just the way you are."

"That's her name?" Celeste asks. "Candy?"

I offer her a proud smile. "Candy Montgomery."

Trenton's eyes double in size.

I snort. "It's okay, big guy. She's in her cage now."

He says something under his breath as he slumps onto the

loveseat with a huff.

"Here's what's going on." Celeste turns to face me. "Last year, Trent had a rough breakup. His fiancé was cheating on him with one of his teammates, who was also his best friend. As you can imagine, things turned ugly."

I frown as I steal a glance at my neighbor. He stares down at his hands while Celeste continues.

"There was a bit of animosity on the team, so the GM traded Trent to the New Jersey Goldfinches, which is why he ended up here as your neighbor."

Anger flashes in my eyes as I lean forward. "Why would they trade you? You weren't the one who messed up the team's dynamic."

Trenton lifts his eyes to mine. "Because I'm older than the other guys on the team and they had a younger goalie waiting in the wings to take my spot."

Damn. His ex left him for a younger man, and his coach dumped him for a younger goalie. The guy might irritate me, but no one deserves to feel like they're not good enough—especially not because of their age.

I scrunch my nose. "That's fucked up. I can see why you've been so grumpy. I'd be slamming doors too if my fiancé got with my best friend."

He grunts. "Right, and my attitude had nothing to do with the musical going on next door to me."

I lift my chin. "You're just lucky I have such good taste in music."

Celeste holds up her hand before he can respond. "So now, Trent has a lot of negative press surrounding him. They're spinning the story to make it sound like Trent was kicked off the team because he couldn't let it go that his friend took his fiancé from him."

I shake my head. "The media sucks."

I'm no stranger to bad reviews, the kind where they go for the jugular instead of stating what they didn't like about the book.

"I'd like to spruce up his image. Show the world that he's not ready for retirement, and that the past is in Seattle because he has a new girlfriend now." A slow smile blooms on her face. "If the world thinks you're dating, then why not let them think that for a while?"

I've read enough fake dating books to know what she's suggesting. "You want us to pretend to date?"

Celeste gives me an eager nod. "I think a few months will suffice. Just enough time for the season to start and for the team to get a few wins under their belt."

I lean back and set my arm on the armrest. "What would I have to do?"

Trenton's mouth falls open. "You're seriously considering this?"

"Why not?"

He shakes his head. "I told Celeste you'd never go for it."

I'm a little shocked myself, but I know that look reflecting in his eyes. If he's feeling anything close to what I've been feeling since I haven't been able to write these last several months, then I'm going to help him get his spark back...and maybe mine in the process.

"Contrary to your opinion, Neighbor Man, I'm a very kind and generous person. I don't mind helping you out, as long as there's something in it for me too."

Celeste squeezes my knee. "Don't worry about that. You'll be generously compensated for your time."

"What? No, I don't want money."

Trenton leans his elbows onto his knees. "You don't?"

"Look around. I'm living in the same apartment as you. I'm a strong independent woman who don't need no man. And if I was that hard up for money, I'd just sell feet pics on the internet like everyone else."

Trenton shoots me a half-glare, half-disgusted look.

Celeste clicks open her pen. "Then what do you want?"

"Three things, and they're nonnegotiable." My mind races as I scoot to the edge of my seat. "One: I get to use parts of this for my next book."

Celeste scribbles it onto her notepad. "Done."

"Hold on a second." Trenton pierces me with an unwavering stare. "You want to write a book about *me*?"

I wave a dismissive hand. "It's not really about you, per se. It's about two characters who live next door to each other and get into a little neighborly dispute."

"That sounds exactly like it's about me."

I roll my eyes. "It's loosely based on you."

"I love it." Celeste beams. "As long as the names are changed, and nothing incriminating goes into the story, then we're all good. What is your second condition?"

"Trenton accompanies me to my high school reunion in February."

He grunts. "You want me to be your dog and pony show?"

I brush off his comment and nod. "Sheldon will be there and since he's part of the reason we're in this mess to begin with, I think it'll be fitting to end it there too."

Celeste's pen flies across the page. "And your third?"

"I get to tell my best friend, Aarya. She's all I have in this world and I'm not lying to her about this."

Celeste slides a paper across the coffee table. "You'll both have to sign an NDA, of course."

Before I take the pen from her, I clear my throat. "Uh, there's actually one more thing I should tell you." I squirm in my seat, my stomach tying itself into knots. "I... I've kind of already been talking about you on TikTok."

Trenton's eyes double in size. "You what?"

"I didn't say your name or anything, because I didn't know your name until today, but I've been telling my followers about my rude new neighbor."

I pull up the initial video on my phone (which now has over one million views) and thrust it into his hand. "Just watch."

It's beyond uncomfortable when someone watches your video right in front of you, forcing you to hear yourself and how ridiculous you sound, but it's an entirely different feeling altogether when the person you're talking about in the video *is* the person watching it.

I can't read Neighbor Man's stoic expression, but Celeste is enthralled.

"This. Is. Perfect." She squeals. "We can totally use this."

"Really? Because I was going to delete it after—"

"No!" She grasps my hand. "Don't delete it. It'll help people get invested in your relationship. It's so authentic."

"It's something all right," Trenton mutters under his breath.

"I'll draw up the papers and have them to you by tonight." Celeste stands and turns to Trenton. "Get her contact information and send it to me."

I arch a brow at Trenton. "You ready for this, Neighbor Man?"

"Are you going to keep calling me that?"

"I'll call you whatever I want. You're my boyfriend now, shnookums."

If looks could kill, I'm pretty sure Trenton's eyes would strike me dead right here on my couch.

At least Celeste thinks I'm funny. Her laughter floats behind her as she scurries out of my apartment, leaving me with my grumpy neighbor.

"We need to start over." I rise from the couch and stick out my hand. "Since we never formally introduced ourselves, no thanks to you, I'm Cassidy Quinn."

He stares at my hand like it's a pesky gnat, but he stands and puts his hand in mine. "Trenton Ward."

I give his mammoth-sized hand a firm shake. "Welcome to the building. There's a gym, a sauna, and the people here are lovely. But be careful, because the doors are really heavy and slam easily."

He squeezes my hand and his nostrils flare. "How thin are the walls? My last neighbor used to blast 80's power ballads before the sun came up."

"I've never had a single complaint." I squeeze his hand right back. "It's *so* nice to meet you."

He can act as irritated as he wants, but I catch the amusement dancing in his eyes when he says, "The pleasure is all mine."

6

TRENTON

"WHY ARE YOU LAUGHING? I thought you were on my side."

Grandma's shoulders shake after I tell her about Cassidy's unhinged TikTok videos. "I *am* on your side. But I think this girl will be good for you. She's got spunk, and you need someone with gumption."

"Gumption." I smirk. "Is that what you call it when someone is a royal pain in the ass?"

She smacks me on the back of my head. "Watch your mouth."

"Ow. How can you still hit as hard as you did when I was a kid?"

"Obviously I'm not hitting you hard enough if you're still using words like that."

I lay back against the chair and smile for what feels like the first time in a really long time. "You know, maybe this whole thing is one big blessing in disguise. I get to spend time with you now that we're living in the same city."

"There's a silver lining in everything bad that happens to you, Trent. It's all about the angle you choose to look at it from."

I cover her hand with mine. "How are you doing?"

"I'm about as well as an eighty-three-year-old woman can be. I told you, don't worry about me. You've got a lot to focus on with preseason around the corner."

"And I told you: I will always worry about you because you're the most important person in my life. Above hockey, above everything."

She shakes her head. "Cassidy is going to fall head over heels in love with you."

I roll my eyes. "This is all fake, Nana. No one's falling in love."

She smiles as if she didn't hear a word I just said, but I won't argue with a senile old woman.

My grandmother falls asleep in her recliner soon after. I linger on the couch, not wanting to leave without saying goodbye to her. I pull up Google on my phone and type in Cassidy's name in the search bar. I don't know what I'm looking for. Celeste did a deep dive on her and came up with nothing more than a speeding ticket several years ago. Cassidy Quinn is a seemingly normal human.

It's pretty impressive that she's a bestselling author. I don't know any authors in real life—especially ones who are only in their twenties. I imagine it's a huge accomplishment.

One of the links takes me to her Instagram account. Most of the posts are about her books, but there are a couple pictures of herself peppered in. I suppose my fake dating situation could be worse. If I have to pretend to date someone, I'm happy it's someone who looks like Cassidy. She's thick and curvy with a killer smile.

If only she didn't get under my skin so much, I would actually be into her.

It's ridiculous that I even have to do this in the first place. I just want to play hockey. Why do I have to worry about my image? Who cares about who I'm dating? Why do any of those things matter? Doesn't the world have anything better to do than gossip?

No matter how many times Celeste explains it to me, I'll never understand it.

I glance over at Nana. *This* is what's important in life. Family. Loved ones. Doing the things you're passionate about.

If people could get off the damn internet and keep their noses out of everyone else's business, the world would be a better place.

AFTER VISITING NANA, I head back to my apartment to do some laundry.

Moving across the country has made all of my clothes wrinkly and smelling like musty cardboard.

A familiar sound floats down the hallway, and I recognize the off-key singing immediately. I slow my stride as I approach the laundry room, and peer through the door that's cracked-open just enough to catch a glimpse of the scene inside.

Cassidy holds a bottle of detergent up to her mouth as she belts out the chorus to Pat Benatar's *Shadows of the Night*. Her hair is tied up in a messy bun on top of her head, and she's dancing around like she's in her own personal laundry room.

An older gentleman glances at her over the top of the book he's trying to read, wearing a small smile on his face.

On the opposite end of the room, a woman taps her foot to the beat of the song.

Does Cassidy not care that people can hear her?

Does she not care that her voice is terrible?

Or is she that oblivious and unaware of her surroundings?

The latter worries me. Carefree crazy is a lot less attractive than delusional crazy.

I carry my laundry bag through the door, and plop it down right next to her. Cassidy yelps when she spins around and spots me.

She taps on her phone and the music stops. "You scared me."

"Didn't think you'd hear me above all that screeching."

She plants her hand on her hip. "What do you have against 80's music?"

"Nothing. It's your rendition of it that I have a problem with."

Her cheeks turn bright-red. "My boyfriend shouldn't speak to me in such a way, you know."

I grunt. "I'll be sure to work on that."

The dryer buzzes and she bends down to pile her clothes into her laundry basket. "I'm going to order in tonight. You should come by so we can discuss our arrangement. Celeste emailed me a schedule of your upcoming calendar and you're about to become a very busy man."

"What is there to discuss?"

"We need to make sure we're on the same page with everything." She lifts a pair of black pants and folds them in half as her eyes dart around the room. "Plus, I have some questions. I don't know anything about hockey, and that seems pretty important since I'm supposed to be dating a hockey player."

I keep forgetting that she doesn't know who I am outside of this building. It's been a while since I've met someone who didn't know me. I guess moving across the country can do that. I've been in a hockey bubble in Seattle for a decade, and I couldn't walk to my car without someone recognizing me or asking for an autograph.

To Cassidy though, I'm simply Neighbor Man who slams his door too hard and makes fun of her singing.

When was the last time I was me, without hockey?

Maybe with her, I can be.

If she's willing to help me then that's the least I can do.

I pour a cap of detergent into the washing machine and toss in my clothes. "What are you ordering?"

"Whatever you want. I'm not picky."

She pulls a scrap of red lace out of her pile and sets it to the side. She continues digging through her clothes until she comes out with a matching bra.

Dear Lord, her body in that set would—no. I'm not picturing my fake girlfriend in her underwear. That wouldn't be right.

Cassidy clears her throat and my eyes flick to hers. "Play your cards right and you'll get to see me in these."

My eyes widen. "What?"

"I'm kidding. Geez, are you this serious all the time?"

Get it together, Ward.

She laughs and shakes her head. "Let's order from Hamilton Pork. Their food is so good, I could go for one of everything on the menu."

I swallow. "I've heard good things about the food here."

Her mouth falls open. "Oh my god, I totally forgot that you're not from around here. I can give you the lowdown on all the best places to eat. Maybe we should go out instead of ordering in. That might be too soon though. I don't think we're ready to look like a couple in public just yet. That'd be a rooky mistake. We definitely need some practice. I've read a lot of books with this trope and they're always unprepared for their first public interactions. You know, it's a good thing you got roped into this mess with me because I actually know a lot about fake dating and..."

She continues rambling on about God-knows-what, but I find my mind drifting back to one singular question.

"Why are you doing this?"

She pauses mid-sentence. "Doing what?"

"This." I gesture between us and lower my voice. "Why are you so willing to fake date someone you don't know? You're not taking the money, and you're already well-known for your books, so you're not in it for the clout. You don't even know who I am, so I can't blame it on you wanting to make another notch in your hockey player belt. So, why, Cassidy Quinn? Why are you helping me?"

She finishes rolling a pair of socks into a ball and tosses them into her basket before hopping up on the washing machine to sit, letting her legs dangle. "Is it so hard to believe that someone wants to do something nice for you?"

"It is when you've been plotting my demise for the last week."

She chuckles, and I try not to notice how nice her smile is. "No one has ever met their demise by out-of-tune singing."

"So you admit you're out-of-tune." I arch a brow. "But I thought your mother used to call you *her little songbird*."

Her eyebrows jump. "You watched *all* of my videos?"

Busted.

I hike a shoulder and act like it's no big deal. "You're a good storyteller."

Her eyes narrow. "You just wanted to hear the part where I said how good-looking you are."

"You can't blame me. That was the only nice thing you said about me in the entire three-part series."

She heaves a sigh and looks into my eyes. "Well, I know what it

40

feels like to be cheated on. To be betrayed by the one person you thought loved you. To not be able to trust anyone afterwards, because if it happened once, it can happen again. To feel like a chump because you didn't see it coming. And if the only way we can get over what happened to us is by getting revenge and pretending to be happy, then I'll do it—for the both of us."

Sadness pricks my heart. Her answer is so real, so raw. It makes me want to be honest with her in return.

I rub the back of my neck before resting my hand on the washing machine beside her. "I'm doing this because I want to show the world that regardless of what happens in my personal life, I'm still a damn-good hockey player. Who I date doesn't matter, what team I'm on doesn't matter, and my age doesn't matter. All that matters is what I leave on the ice."

Cassidy gives me a confident nod. "Then let's show them exactly that."

Warmth rushes over my body, pooling in my chest. It feels good to have someone on my side. When everything went down with my old team, it felt like everyone turned against me. Sure, the team didn't agree with what happened. A guy shouldn't take his best friend's fiancé. But ultimately, I left and no one fought for me to stay. No one stuck up for me but me. I'd never felt so alone before.

Yet here's this stranger who's willing to fabricate a relationship for me. She's willing to step into a whirlwind of professional hockey and paparazzi.

"It isn't easy being picked apart by the world." I pause, not wanting to scare her but needing to warn her for what's to come. "Your life is about to get really public."

She opens her arms wide. "I've got nothing to hide, Neighbor Man. Bring it on."

And I believe her. It's crazy to say that I trust someone I don't even know, but she doesn't seem like the type to be ashamed of anything that could get splashed across the internet. I might not know her, but I'm certain from the few interactions we've had that she owns who she is.

"What can I bring to dinner?"

She lifts the laundry basket and takes a few steps back. "If you want me to be flirty, then bring wine. If you want me to take off my top and dance on the table, then bring tequila. And if you want me to be happy, then bring mint chocolate chip ice cream—the green kind with big chocolate chunks in it."

My eyebrows hit my hairline. "This is a test, isn't it?"

"Choose wisely, Neighbor Man." She winks. "See you at six."

7

CASSIDY

My heart flutters when Trenton arrives promptly at six with a giant carton of mint chocolate chip ice cream.

What a man brings to dinner tells me everything I need to know about him.

I bite my bottom lip to conceal my smile as I stick it inside the freezer. "Interesting choice."

"I figured a happy woman would flirt *and* take off her top, so the ice cream was the best choice to get all three."

I laugh. "That's actually genius. No man has ever given me that response before."

"They all chose wine, didn't they?"

"Most of them did. One man was bold enough to come with tequila, and another brought mint chocolate chip—but it was the white kind."

Trenton wrinkles his nose. "Amateur."

"The food should be here any minute. I hope you don't mind, but I took the liberty of ordering a variety of things. I'm confident you'll love everything."

"Fine by me." He slips his hands into his pockets and glances around my apartment like he's scoping it out.

I take this opportunity to scope *him* out. The ends of his hair look damp, like he towel-dried his hair after he got out of the shower. Slight scruff peppers his jaw, outlining his lips. His dark features only intensify his dark-brown eyes, making them more hypnotic than they already are.

This is the first time I've seen him in jeans, and as much as I like the gray sweatpants, denim looks damn good on him too. The sleeves of his T-shirt stretch around his biceps. His arms are huge; blocky shoulders, round biceps, bulging triceps, and a few prominent veins running down his muscular forearms.

God damn. Is this what all hockey players look like? I've been missing out.

He clears his throat and my eyes snap up to his. "Sorry. I'm a whore for nice arms."

He tilts his head. "You're a what…for what?"

"You know, arm porn." I reach out and squeeze his bicep. "You have really nice arms."

"Oh." He averts his eyes to the floor like he hasn't heard that a thousand times over. "Thanks."

I shrug and pull out a couple of forks from the drawer.

Trenton eyes the bird cage across the room. "Is that thing going to come at me again?"

I stifle a laugh. "She's locked in for the night. Don't worry."

He gives her a hard stare like he doesn't trust her. I guess I won't be telling him about what she did to her poor brother any time soon.

I pull two plates from the cabinet. "So, what is it like being a goalie? That's pretty much the only position I know anything about. You block the goal and that's it, right?"

"In layman terms, sure. I block the goal." He takes the plates from me and sets them down on the table. "But games are won and lost because of the goalie. Everything rides on whether I let a shot get through."

"That sounds like a lot of pressure."

He nods. "It is."

I lean my hip against the counter as I watch him. "I guess out of all the sports, hockey is pretty cool. You're flying across the ice on thin little blades, making the puck go wherever you want it to with a stick. I'm definitely not coordinated enough to do that."

"Have you ever skated?"

I shake my head. "I've never even roller skated, let alone tried it on the ice. It looks hard."

"I guess it is at first. But you get used to it. I've been doing it since I was little. Skating is like second nature to me now."

"It's great that you love what you do."

He leans against the counter, mirroring me. "Do you love being an author?"

"I do. I've always loved writing, ever since I was a kid. My parents fought a lot so I'd hole up in my bedroom with my head-phones and a notebook. I'd make up stories about my life, but I'd make them turn out the way I wanted them to."

"How did they end?"

"Usually with my parents getting hit by a bus or tossed off a cliff."

He sputters. "Really?"

"Don't judge. It was my coping skill."

He grimaces. "I'm guessing they weren't the greatest parents."

"To them, I was just a freeloading nuisance. They definitely didn't plan for me—which they reminded me of every chance they got. I'm honestly surprised they didn't ditch me in a dumpster when they had the chance."

Trenton blinks. "That's…"

"Awful? Yeah." I let out a humorless laugh. "It's fine. I went to therapy and dealt with it. I refuse to be one of those people with mommy and daddy issues who walk around fucking up everyone else's lives with their own damage."

Silence hangs between us, and I fidget with the hem of my shirt. It's not that I *can't* talk about my parents, but the subject makes me uncomfortable because of the pity people impart on me when I tell them.

Poor little girl wasn't loved by her mommy.

A knock at the door gives me an out, so I speed-walk away from the conversation.

I smile when I swing open the door. "Hey, Ru."

Rupert grins. "How's my favorite author doing today?"

I take the brown takeout bag from him. "I wrote part of a chapter today."

"Hey, that's progress."

"Now if I can keep that up, I'll have a whole book."

He lifts his hand and squeezes my shoulder. "The words will be flowing in no time. I know it."

"I hope so." I reach into the bag and pull out a small container. "Here, I got your favorite."

His eyes widen. "No, I can't take your food."

"I ordered it for you, silly. Take it."

He heaves a sigh as he takes the container from me. "Thank you, Miss Cassidy. You're too good to me."

"For you? Never."

He gives me a gracious nod before heading back down the hall.

Trenton watches me with a look of bewilderment. "You do that often?"

"Do what?"

"Order food for the workers here?"

I set down the bag and unload the contents onto the table. "Only for Ru."

He pops open the lid on each container. "Why's that?"

"I wasn't in the best place when I first moved in here. He was so kind and attentive, and he checked on me a lot. You don't find too many compassionate people nowadays. He's a good friend."

"You moved here after your breakup?"

"Yup." I yank on the refrigerator door. "Water, beer, or wine?"

"Water's fine."

I take out two bottles and slide one across the table before dropping into a chair.

I gesture to each container as I rattle off the meals. "This one has a smoky BBQ flavor; this one with the pineapples has a Hawaiian flavor; and if you like sweet and spicy, this sandwich is to die for. But I'll bet you twenty bucks that you'll love the BBQ."

"Why's that?"

"You know that belief where people say dogs look like their owners? Well, I think people enjoy flavors that match their personalities."

He arches a brow. "And my personality says *smoky BBQ guy?*"

The smoking-hot man who's char-grilled and bitter on the outside, but deliciously tender on the inside? Yeah, my money's on BBQ.

I hide my smirk. "Just a hunch."

His eyes narrow on me. "Let me guess: You're sweet and spicy?"

My head tilts back as I let out a laugh. "I'm an easy read."

We're knuckles-deep in pork for the next twenty minutes, grunting like cavemen and barely uttering two words to each other while we eat. This food is that good. It's an experience you don't want to ruin with conversation.

After he finishes off the last of the BBQ pork, he leans back against the chair and sucks his fingers into his mouth one by one, licking them clean of any excess sauce.

I stare with rapt attention, focusing on the way his tongue wraps around the tips of each finger, as well as the rumble of his pleased hum.

Aaaaaaand my panties are soaked.

I need some air.

I gesture to the empty containers scattered around the table. "Leave all this. Let's go sit outside before the sun sets."

I take the carton of ice cream with me, and swipe two spoons from the drawer.

We relax into the pair of lounge chairs I set up on the balcony, letting the sounds of the city below fill the silence.

To my surprise, he speaks first. "So, should I be worried? Are you going to kill me off in your book?"

I flash him a devious smile. "That all depends on how you treat me in real life."

His lips twitch. "Noted."

"We're lucky you know." I hand him a spoon and use mine to carve out a chunk of mint chip. "So many people work because they need a paycheck. They don't love their jobs. They don't have passion for what they do. But we took a hobby and made a living out of it."

"We're definitely doing well for ourselves." He turns to me. "I Googled you. You wrote a lot of books."

I chuckle. "Yeah, I guess so."

"What was Rupert talking about before? Have you been experiencing writer's block?"

"Ever since my breakup." I roll my eyes. "When I caught Sheldon cheating on me, it's as if that moment sucked out all of my romantic mojo or something. Which royally pisses me off because it's like he's still getting the better of me."

Trenton puffs out his cheeks and blows out a long breath through his lips. "It happens. I played like shit when I found out my best friend was screwing my fiancé."

My top lip curls. "That makes me so mad for you. Like why bother getting engaged if you're not fully committed to that person? And your best friend—what kind of friend does that?"

"They're a perfect pair." He stares off into the distance at a point over my shoulder. "Lindsey always wanted me to be more outgoing. Flashier. She wanted to be photographed at all the ritzy places with her Gucci bags. Petroski is the one she should've been with all along because that is so not me."

"Lindsey sounds like a materialistic bitch."

He snorts. "You said it."

"Can I ask...? Why did you propose to her if she wasn't right for you?"

"Honestly, she was pressuring me to get married. The media kept making comments about how old I am, saying it was time to settle down."

"How old are you?"

"Thirty-six."

I roll my eyes. "You're not that old. Plenty of people get married and have kids later in life nowadays."

He nods. "How old are you?"

"Twenty-seven." I shake my head. "I don't get the concept of cheating. Like, just say you're unhappy. Have a conversation like an adult. It's so simple."

He finally digs into the carton for a spoonful of ice cream. "How did you find out about your ex?"

"I walked in on him."

Trenton's eyes widen. "You saw him having sex with another woman?"

"Sure did." A humorless laugh escapes me. "He'd been acting strange for a few weeks. Distant and on his phone a lot. I kept asking him what was wrong and he blamed it on being tired from work. He'd been under a lot of stress at his firm, so I wanted to do something to surprise him and relieve some of his stress. I showed up at his apartment completely naked in a trench coat and heels with a three-course meal that I'd slaved over that day. They were so loud, they didn't even hear me walk in."

He cringes and turns away. "That's fucking awful."

"Every time I try to write a sex scene now, all I can picture is the two of them. I hear the sounds they were making. I see the look on her face. It's like it'll be forever burned into my brain."

"It won't be forever." He pauses. "Can I ask you a forward question?"

"Sure."

"Have you been with anyone since then?"

I shake my head as my cheeks tinge with embarrassment. "Pathetic, huh?"

"Not at all." He shrugs. "I haven't either."

I shoot him a dubious look. "You don't have to lie to make me feel better."

"Why would I lie about that?"

"You're a gorgeous hockey star. I'm sure women throw themselves at you everywhere you go."

"Doesn't mean I take them up on it."

I side-eye him, searching for a sign that he's lying. All I find is an honest pair of brown eyes.

"I think once you're with someone else, you'll have new material for your sex books."

I laugh. "They're not just about sex."

He arches a brow. "How explicit are the scenes?"

"You should read one and find out."

"Okay."

My eyebrows shoot up to my hairline. "Really?"

"Sure. Tell me which one you recommend and I'll read it. I'll need something to do while I'm traveling for away games."

The idea of Trenton reading my book fills me with excitement. I already know which one I'm going to give him.

I shovel a heaping spoonful of ice cream into my mouth. "You know what? Just because we're pretending to be together doesn't mean we have to pretend to be happy. I say let's have fun with this." I pause. "You know how to have fun, don't you?"

He smirks. "Yes, smartass." Then he brings his eyes to meet mine and hold my gaze. "Thank you, by the way. I realize I never said it. Thanks for doing this for me."

"I've got your back now, Neighbor Man." I clink my spoon against his. "Lucky for you."

8

CASSIDY

THE COLD AIR hits my nose as soon as we step through the curtain.

I pause on the stairs to take a video panning around the stadium.

"Wait until the season starts," Celeste says. "This place will be packed."

I slip my phone back into my purse and hold onto the railing as we descend into the stadium. "What's the difference between preseason and the actual season?"

"Preseason is like a bunch of practice games. New players get to try out for specific positions, and the coach gets to evaluate his players. Not every player will make the big club."

"The big club...?"

"You know, the NHL. Coaches want only the best players to start the game." She smiles. "Trent's really good, Cass. Wait until you see what he can do."

"Good. I hope his old team regrets trading him."

She chews her bottom lip. "I'm worried about that game. They'll have to play each other at some point, and I have a feeling it's going to be ugly."

My stomach sours at the thought of him playing against his asshole ex-best friend.

We take our seats in front of the glass, and I snap some pictures while we wait for the warmup to start.

"I can't believe you've never been to a hockey game before." Celeste nudges me with her shoulder. "I'm excited to pop your cherry."

"I'm glad you're my first." I smile. "It feels good to get out and try something new. Being a writer, I tend to be holed up in my apartment a lot."

"How's the new story coming along?"

"I have the basics of the beginning down." I take a swig of my soda. "I'm excited to dive into the hockey aspect. I love researching new topics to write about."

She flips her auburn hair over her shoulder. "Just make sure the hockey player's PR agent is super-hot."

I toss my head back as I laugh. "Don't worry, I got you."

Music blares over the loudspeakers, and colored lights swirl over the ice from above. Butterflies swarm my belly. It'll be interesting to see Trenton in his element. I'm excited to see this side of him. I need to crack him open and dive inside to learn more about him if I'm going to do his character justice. Watching him play seems like the perfect place to start.

The announcer introduces the Goldfinches, and soon they're gliding over the ice, circling each other like a frenzy of sharks in the water. I take out my phone and record them, searching for Trenton.

"There he is." Celeste points to the number one on his black and yellow jersey. "Normally, we'll sit behind his goal, but I wanted you to have a full view of the rink today."

Trenton might be two-hundred-pounds, but he flies over the ice like he's featherlight. His gear is slightly different than the other players, with large pads over his legs and a cage over his face instead of a clear shield. I zoom in to record him as he skates around.

He makes his way around the perimeter of the rink, but slows down as he approaches where we're sitting.

"Let's go, Ward!" Celeste shouts.

I can't make out his expression through the face mask, but his eyes find mine and he shoots me a wink before skating away.

Celeste leans in. "Tell me you got that on video."

I glance down at my phone and fight the smile tugging at my lips.

"Make sure you post that." She sits back against her seat with a devilish smile. "Puck bunnies will eat that shit up."

"Puck bunnies?"

"Every sport has them. Jersey chasers, buckle bunnies, cleat chasers. They're like groupies who just want to say they fucked a professional athlete."

"Ah. Got it." I open the notes app on my phone and type that in for future reference.

"Trent has a huge fanbase. He does volunteer work and donates to charities. He's a great role model to kids. You should see him with them." Her eyes light up. "In fact, you should attend some events with him. I'll set it up soon and email you the dates."

I chuckle. "Does your brain ever stop thinking about work?"

"Literally never."

Some of the players bend down to stretch their legs, moving from side to side. Others are stick-handling a puck pretend to push an imaginary hockey puck, moving their stick back and forth.

But my eyes fixate on Trenton because he's kneeling on the ice with his legs spread wide, performing what I can only imagine is a sexual maneuver as he humps the air.

My mouth falls open. "What the hell is he doing?"

Celeste cackles. "He's a goalie, so he needs to make sure his groin is stretched for optimal mobility. He's in a squat position for most of the game."

"Damn," I murmur. I press record and shamelessly stare as he swirls his knees in circles and continues to gyrate on the ice. It's physically impossible to think of anything other than Trenton having sex while he's moving like this. And in my head, I'm underneath him.

That makes two times now that Trenton has made me wet without even trying.

This is going to be a problem.

When Trenton finishes his stretches, he heads to the net and goes through a series of repetitive movements that look like he's blocking an imaginary puck from the goal.

One of the players on the opposing team from New York skates to the red line in the center of the rink, spraying ice as he skids to a stop. I can't make out what he says over the music, but several of Trenton's teammates glance back at him to wait for his reaction. Trenton shakes his head and continues practicing, but one of his teammates—Krumkachova, number sixteen—skates to the line to meet the opposing player. Words are exchanged, and judging by their body language, they aren't having a friendly chat. Then, Krumkachova skates around to the goal and pats Trenton on the pads before skating away.

"Wow."

I glance at Celeste. "What just happened there?"

"That asshole on the other team must've been trash talking Trenton." She points to his teammate wearing number eighteen. "But he stuck up for him. That's promising. We need this new team to accept him."

The corners of my lips tug into a frown. "Does he get that a lot, people being mean to him?"

"Chirping is part of the game. But Trenton stays out of fights. You're not supposed to touch the other team's goalie, so everyone usually respects that."

"Fights?"

Celeste nods. "They're allowed to fight every now and then in hockey. You'll see."

"Sports are so weird."

She laughs. "You're going to learn so much, my little grasshopper."

After sixteen minutes of warming up, both teams head back into their locker rooms until the game starts.

Trenton doesn't play for the entire game, which is typical for a starter during the preseason according to Celeste, but I eat up every second he's on that ice. The agility, the talent, the speed in which he blocks each shot...it's impressive. My shoulders jerk up to my ears every time the puck slams into the wall with crazy force, and I wonder how much of it Trenton feels through his padding and gloves.

The team wins 2-0 and I give that asshole on the opposing team a mental middle finger.

"So, what did you think of your first game?" Celeste asks.

"It was fun. I had no idea what was going on half the time but I got excited when they scored a point."

Celeste laughs. "It's called a *goal*. We have to teach you some hockey lingo."

On our way out of the stadium, someone shouts my name. I turn around and the bright flash of a camera blinds me.

"Cassidy, why aren't you wearing Ward's jersey?"

"Is this just a PR stunt?"

"How is Trenton feeling on the new team?"

Celeste wraps her arm around my shoulders and guides me outside. "Don't say anything. Let's go."

Several men chase after us as we scurry through the parking lot, and they continue snapping pictures of us until we drive away.

I blink several times and glance at Celeste in the driver's seat. "Jesus."

"Just wait until the season starts." She says it like I'm supposed to be excited about it. "I'll prepare some answers for you so you're not thrown off when you're approached by reporters."

"One of them asked if we were fake dating. Do you think this is going to be believable?"

She flips her blinker on. "You two have to go on a date. Get out there in public. The more they see you together, the more they'll buy it."

I let my head fall back against the headrest while Celeste tells Siri a list of tasks she needs to be reminded of. And a small shiver of anticipation shimmies down my spine at the thought of going on a date with Trenton.

Those goalie exercises are really messing with my head.

It's late when a light knock taps against my door.

Excitement squeezes my stomach. I was hoping Trenton would stop by when he got back from the game, but I wasn't holding my breath.

I step back and wave him inside with the wine glass in my hand. "Hey, great game."

"Thanks." He shoves his hands into his pockets and I try not to stare too intently at the bulge outlined in his sweatpants. "Celeste said the reporters were hassling you. I just wanted to make sure you were okay."

I wave a dismissive hand. "It wasn't a big deal. It did get me thinking though. One of them asked if our relationship was a PR stunt, so we need to make this believable."

He tilts his head. "What do you have in mind?"

I dart across the room and swipe the notebook off my desk. "I've been making a list of all the things we need to do to make this look legit." I flip open to the page and hand it to him. "These are the basics, but you can add anything you think might help."

Trenton's eyes move over the short list.

1. Go on a date
2. Hold hands in public
3. Post pictures on social media
4. Kiss

"These are the things real couples do, so we should be doing them too."

He nods. "Okay."

"Hey, what did that guy from the other team say to you during warmups?"

Trenton lifts his hand and rubs the back of his neck. "Ah, nothing. Just talking shit."

"What did he say?"

His eyes bounce around the room until they finally settle on mine. "He said, *You must love losing—you lost your girl and your team.*"

My lips pull down into a frown. "What an asshole."

"It's all part of the game. Players are going to try to get into my head." He shrugs. "Obviously it didn't work because my team won."

"Celeste said you're allowed to fight during the game. I think you should beat someone's ass and teach them a lesson." I slap my bicep. "Or just send him my way and I'll show him what's up."

He chuckles. "You're my bodyguard now?"

I lift my chin. "If I have to be. Nobody talks about my boyfriend like that."

He shakes his head. "Nothing anyone says could ever be worth getting into a fight. That's all part of the show for the crowd. I just want to play."

"Oh! That reminds me." I bite my lip to conceal my smile as I unlock my phone and pull up the TikTok video I created earlier. "You're going viral."

I may or may not have posted the video I took of him performing his goalie warmups.

The corner of his mouth twitches as he watches himself hump the ice. "The song is a nice touch."

I grin. "I thought so."

Pony by Ginuwine, of course.

"Leave it to the romance author to turn my stretches into a sexual thing."

I scoff, feigning offense. "Are you calling me a pervert?"

"If the shoe fits."

"You're the one gyrating like an exotic male dancer, okay? You can't blame a girl for noticing." I take a sip of wine. "Now the real question is: Do you have the size to back it up, or do you rely on the motion of your ocean?"

He eyes my wine glass and his lips curve into a smirk. "Feeling flirty, are we?"

I hike a nonchalant shoulder. "I'm just saying, you look like you've got skills."

He leans down and his lips brush against my ear. "Cassidy Quinn, you have no idea."

I stand there for several minutes after he walks out of my apartment.

That makes three.

Three times this man has caused me to change my underwear.

I've gotta up my game.

9

TRENTON

"Is this Trenton Ward?"

"Yes. Is everything okay?"

"Your grandmother took a bit of a spill. We're having an ambulance come to take her to the hospital."

I jump up from my bed. "What happened?"

"She must have fallen getting out of bed. We found her on the floor, and it looks like she may have broken her nose. But she's conscious and coherent."

I throw on a T-shirt and race to get dressed. "Which hospital?"

"Jersey City Medical Center. I'll let them know that you'll meet her there."

"Thank you."

I grab my keys and shove my feet into a pair of slides. When I rip open the door, I barrel straight into Cassidy.

She gives me a bright smile. "Hey, I was just coming to tell you —what's wrong?"

"My grandmother is being rushed to the hospital."

Cassidy follows me down the hallway. "What happened?"

"They said she fell out of bed. Maybe a broken nose." I slap the button for the elevator. "How far is Jersey City Medical Center?"

"Five minutes. I can take you there."

"You don't have to do that."

Cassidy steps inside the elevator with me when the door opens. "I'm coming with you either way, and I know where it is so you might as well let me drive."

I nod. "Thank you."

Tears sting the backs of my eyes as I imagine my grandmother falling and not knowing where she is or how to ask for help. How long was she lying there until they found her? How much pain is she in? Does she even understand what's happening?

Cassidy reaches out and clasps my hand. "They can fix a broken nose. She's going to be okay."

"She has Alzheimer's so I don't know if she understands what's going on." I swallow. "Sometimes she gets confused and she can give people a hard time when they're trying to help her."

"We'll be there soon."

I squeeze her hand, thankful to have her by my side.

Cassidy weaves through traffic like a NASCAR driver and gets us to the hospital within minutes. She leads us in through the emergency entrance and helps me fill out the necessary paper-work, and when the nurse calls my name, I use my *I'm a famous hockey player* status to convince her to let the both of us back together.

I rush over to my grandmother's bedside, my heart wrenching at the sight of the bruises forming under each puffy eye.

"Nana, are you okay?"

"I'm fine." She waves a dismissive hand. "You didn't need to come here."

"Of course I did. You're hurt. Did the nurse give you anything for the pain?"

"I don't know what she did. I was poked and prodded and I have this stupid tube in my hand." She lifts her left hand to show me. "Hurts like a bitch."

"Do you know how you fell?"

"I think my leg got tangled in the blanket. I went to get out of bed and then I just fell." Nana's eyes glance over my shoulder. "Oh, my. Who is this you have with you?"

"This is Cassidy." I turn around and wave her into the room. "She's the girl I was telling you about."

"You were talking about me? That can't be good." Then Cassidy's eyebrows hit her hairline. "Oh my god, Sherry?"

Nana's eyes narrow as Cassidy gets closer. "Birdie, is that you?"

Birdie?

Cassidy moves past me and clutches Nana's hand. "You're Trent's grandmother."

I tilt my head. "You know each other?"

"She was my neighbor before you moved in." Cassidy presses a kiss to the top of Nana's hand. "I was so worried about you."

Nana smiles wide. "It's so good to see you again."

"I miss our card games."

I lower myself to the edge of the hospital bed as it all sinks in.

Cassidy *is* Birdie.

Cassidy befriended Nana and took care of her when I couldn't be here.

It was difficult being all the way across the country, unable to ensure that my grandmother was taken care of. But knowing she had someone in the building to look after her was comforting.

"Every Tuesday and Thursday, we played Rummy." Cassidy beams up at me. "She'd bake the most delicious desserts and we'd listen to music."

Appreciation settles into my chest. "I remember. She told me about you. I just can't believe I didn't put it together sooner."

Cassidy shoots me a harmless glare. "Your grandson doesn't like my singing, Sherry. Did he tell you that?"

Nana scoffs. "No, he most certainly did not. Trenton, you better behave yourself. My Birdie is a sweet girl."

I arch a brow. "*Your* Birdie? But I'm your grandson."

"And my grandson is going to be kind to my friend."

Cassidy sticks out her tongue and then shoots me a wink.

I can't help but smirk.

Cassidy keeps Nana in good spirits until the doctor comes in to go over the x-rays, and I'm relieved to hear that it's no more than a fractured nose.

We take her back to the nursing home and I stay with her until visiting hours come to an end.

"I love you, Nana. Get some rest. I'll be back to check on you tomorrow."

"I love you too sweetheart." Nana glances up and spots Cassidy standing in the doorway, and her expression changes. "Trenton, you didn't tell me you had a friend with you. Who is that?"

My eyebrows press together. "That's Cassidy. Birdie, your old neighbor...remember? She was just with us at the hospital."

Nana tilts her head. "Why were we at the hospital? Are you hurt?"

"No. You fell. Don't you remember?"

"I didn't fall. I'm fine."

I lift my eyes to Cassidy, and she just gives me a sad smile.

We say goodbye, and head back to the apartment.

"While you were with your grandmother, I spoke with the director of the facility about getting a remote-controlled bed with rails." Cassidy glances at me before returning her eyes to the road. "This way, she can hold onto something while she gets in and out of bed, and it won't be so high off the ground."

My lips part in surprise. "That's a great idea. What did she say?"

"She said it'd be expensive but something they could definitely accommodate." Cassidy switches on the blinker and rolls to a stop at the light. "I told her that money is not a problem, and we'd like more information on how to go about getting a bed for her as soon as possible. So, be on the lookout for an email from her."

I swallow. "Thank you for doing that."

"I also told them we want more frequent checks on her since we know she's a fall risk. Who knows how long she was lying there before someone came to check on her."

Cassidy asked questions I didn't even think of while I was making sure Nana was comfortable and settled in her room. I didn't have to ask for her help. I didn't have to say a word. She was by my side without a second thought.

"I love that woman." Cassidy smiles while she shakes her head.

"She was one of my dearest friends when she lived next door. I can't believe she's your grandmother. What a small world."

"It really is crazy how neither of us realized it."

"And you know what else I was thinking about? Your grandmother called me Birdie, obviously because I have a bird. But you got traded to the Goldfinches, which is a bird." She smacks the steering wheel. "What are the odds of that? It's like all of this was somehow meant to be."

I chuckle and entertain her theory. "Yeah, maybe you're right."

"You don't believe in that stuff, do you?"

"I don't know." I let my head fall back against the headrest. "I think our paths crossed because I took my grandmother's apartment next door to you. I don't read into anything that much."

She hums. "Well, either way, I'm glad your grandmother is okay."

Cassidy pulls into the parking garage and puts the car in park, but neither of us makes a move to exit the car.

"Thank you for coming with me today." I shift in the seat to face her. "I know she was happy to see you, even if the moment was fleeting."

She chews her bottom lip. "I'd like to continue visiting her, if that's okay with you."

"Of course. She'd love that."

"I don't have any family of my own." She laughs. "I guess if you're my fake boyfriend, then she can be my fake grandmother, right?"

Sadness grips my chest. "You don't talk to your parents?"

"When I hit the New York Times Bestseller list for the first time, they came around looking for a handout." She lets out a humorless laugh. "They didn't come to congratulate me or celebrate. They just wanted to use me. I was young and stupid, and I gave them a little bit of money thinking they'd leave me alone after that. But it wasn't enough. They blew through it, probably on drugs or at the casino, and then they tried coming back for more. I haven't heard from them in eight years."

I reach out and cover her hand with mine. "It's their loss."

"They don't see it that way. And that's okay. My friends are my family." Cassidy stares down at our clasped hands. "My parents taught me how to take care of myself, so I'm grateful for that."

Leave it to her to put a positive spin on her asshole parents.

Something stirs inside of me—something fierce and protective. She took care of Nana, so I'm going to make sure Cassidy is taken care of too. It's the least I can do to repay her.

"For what it's worth, you're not alone, Cassidy Quinn. You have me now."

She chuckles. "I know, it's part of the contract."

My eyebrows press together. "Hey, look at me."

She lifts her hazel eyes to mine.

"You have me, regardless of the contract. If you need something, don't hesitate to ask. You understand?"

She nods, and a small smile touches her lips. "Got it, Neighbor Man."

10

TRENTON

"COME IN!"

I crack open the door to Cassidy's apartment and peer into the living room.

"I'm almost ready," she calls from another room. "Just putting on the last-minute touches."

My stomach churns. Nerves have been eating away at me since Celeste set up the details of our date. I hate making a spectacle out of something that should be normal. I hate knowing the paparazzi will be watching our every move, knowing that our pictures will be splashed across the news pages by tomorrow.

Most of all, I hate that I've dragged Cassidy into this circus. She didn't ask for this. She didn't seek out a professional athlete to fake date. I know how cruel people on the internet can be, and I can't protect her from the things they might say. They can say whatever they want about me, but I don't want them hurting her.

I walk over to the tall bookshelf by the window, but freeze when I spot the bird cage. The door is open, and the beady-eyed little ball of feathers hops along her perch, moving closer to the opening.

I creep toward the cage. "Don't come out. Stay right there."

She tilts her head as if she's contemplating it.

"Don't bite off my finger." I reach out and lift the lever. "I'm just closing the door." I slide the door until it reaches the bottom, and hook the latch. "That's a good girl."

"Who's a good girl?"

I spin around at the sound of Cassidy's voice. "I was talking to—"

The words die on my tongue.

Maroon lace hugs her breasts, the neckline cutting low in a deep V. She's in skin-tight high-waisted jeans with even higher maroon heels on. Her eyes are lined with a thin swipe of black and her hair cascades down around her shoulders in loose curls. My gaze lingers on her plump lips, painted as dark as her shirt.

Jesus Christ. This woman is every one of my fantasies come to life. Voluptuous and sexy as hell while still leaving things to the imagination.

And I have a good fucking imagination.

"I feel like I'm all tits and ass, but I kind of like it." She turns around and pulls her hair over her shoulder, looking back at her ass. "Is it too much?"

Too much? Is she kidding me?

"It's the perfect amount." I clear my throat. "You look unbelievable."

Her eyebrows jump as a pink flush crawls into her cheeks. "Thanks."

I gesture to the bookshelf, needing to take my mind and my eyes off of her body before I have to explain why my pants suddenly grew tighter around my dick. "Pretty cool to have a shelf filled with your own books."

"I love it even more when I see my books on other people's shelves. I imagine it's the same feeling you get when you see people wearing your jersey."

"Yeah, it's a great feeling."

The image of Cassidy wearing my number flashes in my mind, and it's suddenly very hot in this room.

I jerk my thumb toward the bird cage. "Hope you don't mind, I shut the door."

She giggles. "Why are you so afraid of her?"

"I don't like anything with wings."

"Not even butterflies?"

"Not even butterflies."

"What if it can't fly, like a penguin or a chicken?"

"Penguins don't count. But I don't fuck with chickens."

She shakes her head. "You're so peculiar."

"Says the one who named her bird after an axe murderer."

Cassidy stands in front of the cage and sticks her finger inside. The bird hops along the perch until she reaches Cassidy, and then bows her head.

Cassidy scratches the top of her head with her index finger. "See? She's a sweetie."

"I'll take your word for it." I heave a sigh and square my shoulders. "You ready for this?"

She waves her arm in a grand flourish. "I'm ready for my acting debut."

The usual paparazzi are camped out outside our apartment building, but it's nothing compared to the throng of cameras flashing outside the restaurant.

"Celeste said she was going to leak our location to a couple of people." I peel my eyes from the crowd outside the car window. "I think she needs to brush up on her math if this is what she calls *a couple*."

"She's just trying to help." Cassidy reaches over and squeezes my hand. "We've got this."

"I'm going to come around and open your door. Stay close, okay?"

She nods and takes a deep breath.

Everyone shouts my name as soon as I step out of the car. I race around the front end and yank open the door, reaching for Cassidy. I wrap my arm around her shoulders and tuck her against me, trying to shield her from the camera flashes.

We get inside and the hostess ushers us to our seat in a small corner booth.

Cassidy scoots in first and I slide in beside her. Her eyes are wide, darting from window to window as the paparazzi gather outside.

"I'll have the shades closed," says the hostess.

"Thank you so much." I offer her a polite smile. "I appreciate it."

I place my hand over Cassidy's bouncing knee. "You okay?"

"Yeah, that was just...a lot." She lets out a chuckle. "You really experience this everywhere you go?"

"Not everywhere. I think it's like this because I'm new here and they're able to get the first scoop on our story."

She hums. "I'd never want that job. It's so intrusive."

"Me neither."

Once the waitress comes and takes our drink orders, Cassidy seems back to her normal talkative self.

The only problem is, I can't stop staring at her mouth.

"What made you want to be a goalie? Why not be a... wingman or something?"

I cover my mouth with my fist as I laugh into it. "It's not wingman. It's left wing and right wing."

She waves her water glass in the air. "Whatever, you know what I mean."

I do know what she means. She's trying, and it's adorable.

"Well, I remember the first time I learned what hockey was. My mom used to take me to work with her every Saturday. She owned a candy shop and I loved helping her melt the chocolate and pour it into the molds. She'd always let me take a few home after.

"At the time, there was an ice-skating rink being built on the next street over. When it was finally done, my mom took me over there after her shift one day so I could check it out. There was a high school hockey game taking place, and I remember being mesmerized by the way those kids flew across the ice. I immediately told my mom I wanted to play hockey—I was seven years old—and I pointed to the goalie. She asked why the goalie, and I said, *because he never leaves the ice.* All the other players would come in and out of the game, but the goalie stayed in the whole time."

I pause and take a sip of water. "Honestly, I wasn't that good when I started skating. I had a difficult time balancing on the skates, and I wasn't as fast as the other guys. So I guess it's a good thing I had my heart set on being a goalie because I wouldn't have made it in any other position."

Cassidy listens with rapt attention, propping up her head in her hand with her elbow on the table. "Where does your mom live now?"

"She passed about ten years ago. She had a tough battle with breast cancer."

Cassidy touches her fingers to her lips. "I'm so sorry, Trent."

"Thanks. She was the greatest person I've ever known."

"Do you have any pictures of her?"

I scroll through the photos on my phone. "Here's a few from when I was younger."

"Oh, my God. You were such a chunker."

I chuckle. "And this was later on when I got drafted to the NHL."

"She was so beautiful. You have her smile." Cassidy pauses. "What about your dad?"

"Never knew him. My mom was casually dating a guy in college and when he found out she was pregnant, he dumped her."

She gasps. "What an asshole."

I hike a shoulder. "I've done just fine all these years without him."

"Yes, you have. That's amazing you knew what you wanted to do from such a young age. And it all worked out. Look at you now."

I let out a bitter laugh. "Yeah, look at me. I was traded from one of the best teams and betrayed by my best friend."

She sits up ramrod straight. "Hey, don't focus on that shit. You're still in the NHL and you're getting to play the game you love. You're lucky. Imagine if you had a career-ending injury and you could never play again, or if no other team wanted you." She jabs her finger at me. "You have an opportunity here, and you're going to rock it. So, stop replaying what happened in the past, and look at what's ahead of you. Those assholes did you a favor, and now you're going to mop the floor with them. Or the ice, I guess. But you don't really mop ice, so that wouldn't make sense. You're going to annihilate them this season. You're going to win the... the trophy. The big silver cup thing. And they'll be sorry they let you go. You're——"

I lean in and cut her off with a kiss.

I'm just as surprised as she is, and we both pause with our lips pressed together.

Shit, why did I do that? I should've asked first.

But Cassidy doesn't pull away. She tilts her head and parts her lips, slipping her tongue inside my mouth in search of mine. My hands weave into her hair, gripping the silky strands at the base of her head to hold her where I want her.

Every nerve ending in my body sparks to life. This isn't a demure peck on the lips. This isn't a kiss for the cameras. It's unexpected and all-consuming—and hot as hell.

Cassidy sighs into my mouth, and the sound is nearly my undoing. I feel that soft whimper of need like it's my own, and if we weren't in the middle of a restaurant right now, I'd give her what she wants.

I pull back first, but not without sucking on her bottom lip and releasing it with a pop. Her hair is tousled from my hands and her lipstick smeared, but it only makes my dick harder to see her like this.

Fuck, I need to get my mind out of the gutter when I'm around this woman.

Her cheeks flush as her eyes dart around the restaurant. "Do you think anyone saw us?"

"To be honest, I don't really care."

"And why's that?"

"I didn't kiss you for them."

"Then why did you?"

"Because I couldn't wait one more second to find out what you taste like."

She visibly shivers and her gaze drops to my mouth. "I—"

"Here are your drinks. Sorry for the wait." The waitress sets down my beer and Cassidy's wine glass. "Do you have any questions about the menu, or are you ready to order?"

"We haven't even looked at the menu yet." Cassidy smooths

down her hair and gives the waitress a sheepish smile. "I'm sorry. Do you mind coming back in a few minutes?"

"Of course not. Take your time." She pauses and turns her attention to me. "I hope I'm not intruding, but my son is a huge hockey fan. Do you think I could have your autograph for him?"

"Absolutely. Would you like to FaceTime him?"

Her mouth drops open. "Oh my god, I would win mother of the year if you called him right now." She scrambles to pull out her cell phone. "His name is Toby, and he's eight-years-old."

Toby answers his mother's call after a couple of rings. "Baby, look who I have here at the restaurant with me."

She turns her phone and I take it from her grasp. "Hi, Toby."

The little boy's eyes light up. "Wow, you're Trenton Ward!"

I chuckle. "I am. I heard you're a big hockey fan."

He nods eagerly. "I want to be a goalie like you when I grow up."

"That's fantastic. Keep practicing and listen to your mom, and I'm sure you'll get there one day."

We talk for a few more minutes while he shows me his bedroom and the hockey posters on his wall. Then his mom takes back her phone and says goodnight.

"Thank you so much for doing that. It really means a lot to me." She dabs the corner of her eye with her pinky. "Toby has been getting bullied by some kids at school. They know we don't have a lot of money, and his father walked out when he was a baby, so they're making him feel bad about it."

My heart wrenches in my chest. "I was raised by a single mom and we didn't come from much either, so I get it."

"Really? Oh, I'll make sure to tell him that. He's going to love knowing you have something in common."

I lean over and pull out my phone from my pocket. "Why don't you put your number in my phone. I live right here in town, and I'd love to come visit Toby's school and meet my buddy in person."

Tears stream down her face. "Are you serious? You'd do that?"

"Of course." I hand her my phone and she types her number into it before handing it back to me. "My schedule is a little hectic now that preseason has started, but I'll do my best to fit some time for Toby into the next week or two. We'll show those bullies who the cool kid really is."

She wipes her cheek with the back of her hand and sniffles. "Thank you so much, Mr. Ward. Truly, you have no idea how much I appreciate this."

"Absolutely."

She glances at Cassidy. "I'm so sorry to intrude on your date night like this. Please, take your time with the menu. I'll come back in a little to check on you."

Cassidy reaches out and takes her hand. "Don't be sorry. I'm so glad we came here tonight. It's like this was meant to be."

After the waitress walks away, Cassidy dips her head and dabs her eye with the corner of her napkin.

I curl her hair behind her ear and tip her face to look at me. "Hey, are you okay?"

She nods. "That was just so sweet. You made that mother's whole year, and you're going to help that little boy."

"I hate hearing about kids getting bullied."

She reaches up and presses her palm against my cheek. "You're a good man, Trenton Ward."

I lean into her touch, gazing into her eyes and letting myself get lost in them. Affection pulls at my heartstrings.

"And you're a damn good kisser, Cassidy Quinn."

She grins and waggles her eyebrows. "Yeah, I am."

"So modest too."

She throws her head back and laughs.

I laugh too, and I can't help but wonder if Cassidy was right.

Maybe everything is somehow meant to be. All of this. Maybe our paths were destined to cross. And in this particular moment, I'm not so mad about it, even after everything that has happened.

I don't think there's anywhere else I'd rather be right now than beside Cassidy in this restaurant.

11

CASSIDY

"What happened when you guys got back to your apartment at the end of the night?"

I groan. "He walked me to my door and said goodnight."

"What?" Aarya shrieks so loud I hold the phone away from my ear. "No kiss? No hot hockey player sex?"

"Nope. I honestly feel like we both knew if we kissed in proximity to a bed, we'd cross a line that we couldn't uncross." I let out an audible sigh. "I'm telling you, dude. We had major chemistry. Like, that kiss was the best kiss I've ever had in my entire existence. That man has ruined me for all other kisses. And the whole thing with the little boy and his mother? God, I'm surprised I didn't start undressing in the middle of the restaurant and ask him to take me right then and there."

"I've been doing some research on him and the guy seems like a real class act, Cass. If you like him and he likes you, what would be so bad about crossing that line?"

I stare up at the sky and watch the clouds pass overhead. "This isn't a real thing. This is temporary. I signed a freaking contract, for crying out loud. Wouldn't that make me a prostitute?"

"You're not getting paid for it. Stop. And just because it's a fake setup doesn't mean something real isn't happening between you."

"I know. But we just started this whole thing. I don't want to throw a monkey wrench into it and ruin everything."

"Well, just keep an open mind and an open heart. You never know what could happen."

I know she's right, but after everything I went through with Sheldon, I'm scared to open up my heart to someone new.

"Have you heard from him today?" Aarya asks.

"No." I fight a frown, refusing to feel upset about not waking up to a text from my fake boyfriend.

"All right, that's it. Let's get you out for a little bit. Meet me for lunch. Tacos will make everything better."

"Fine, but no margaritas. I have to write some more when I get back."

"Deal."

I head inside and change out of my sweats. I usually don't get dressed up for lunch dates with Aarya, but now that the paparazzi knows where I live, I don't want to look like a ragamuffin. I settle on an outfit in between the two, and throw on ripped shorts and a Led Zeppelin T-shirt. Then I grab my purse off the entryway table and swing open my door.

Sitting on the floor in the hallway is a bouquet of big pink flowers.

What the heck?

I crouch down to read the note attached to it.

Good Morning,
The woman at the flower shop said peonies are a symbol of happiness and beauty. I figured they were perfect for you. Thank you for dealing with the cameras and flashing lights last night. I hope you got enough material to do some writing today. I got you a little something for the game tonight. See you there.
—Neighbor Man

THERE's a small bag beside the flowers, and I smile when I pull out a black and yellow hockey jersey—with four bold letters across the back: WARD.

The flowers and the letter are a surprisingly romantic gesture. I tap out a text to Trenton before bringing everything inside.

Me: The flowers are beautiful. Thank you.

Neighbor Man: Have you seen the pictures from last night?

Neighbor Man: *insert picture*

Me: We look cute.

Neighbor Man: I wouldn't call your outfit "cute" but yes, we do.

Me: Wait until you see me in your jersey later *wink emoji*

Neighbor Man: I'm looking forward to it.

Me: I'm looking forward to watching you hump the ice again.

Neighbor Man: Pervert.

Me: You like it.

Neighbor Man: I do.

TRENTON'S TEAM won their second game.

I got home over an hour ago, but I'm still in his jersey, waiting for him to come back from the stadium. He doesn't have to stop by to check in with me, but I'm hoping he wants to. He also didn't have to get me flowers this morning yet the beautiful bouquet is in a vase on my desk.

I haven't been able to get our kiss out of my head. I squeeze my thighs together, trying to subdue the ache between them. It's been so long since I've felt another man's touch, I didn't realize how badly I've been craving it.

An idea sparks in my head.

It's crazy, but so is fake dating a pro hockey player.

No, I can't ask him to do that...

Can I?

A knock sounds at the door and I peek through the peephole even though I know who it is. A freshly showered Trenton stands tall in the hallway, sporting gray sweats and a white T-shirt.

His eyes drop to the jersey swallowing up my body, and several silent seconds pass between us. Then his mouth is on mine. He fists my jersey, bunching it up around my hips as he spins us and pins me against the door to close it.

My toes barely touch the floor as I stretch up to reach him, until he lifts me up and holds me in his arms. My legs wrap around him and my hands snake around the back of his neck, tugging at the roots of his damp hair.

His tongue sweeps inside my mouth, deepening the kiss, and I struggle to keep my hips from rolling against him. His massive hands are splayed across my ass, squeezing hard, digging his fingers into my bare skin under my thin sleep shorts.

Our kiss is frantic and urgent, filled with lust and need.

And God to I want more.

He trails kisses down my jaw and along my neck, biting at the sensitive skin. "Seeing you wearing my jersey does something to me."

"I'll wear it all the time if this is how you're going to react."

I can feel his hardness through his sweats, and my control slips as I rub myself against him.

"Fuck, Cassidy." His voice is hoarse and strained as he nips at my collar bone. "I don't know what you're doing to me."

I trace his ear with my tongue. "I know what I'd *like* to do to you."

He drops his forehead to mine, and his ragged breaths graze my lips. "Should we stop?"

"I don't know. Do you want to stop?"

He presses his erection against me. "Does it feel like I want to stop?"

I grin. "Let's talk. I have an idea I want to run by you."

Trenton places me down, and straightens my jersey for me.

Then I clasp his hand and lead him to the couch. I sit a safe distance away from him leaving a cushion between us, but he pulls me closer and takes my legs onto his lap like he can't help but touch me.

I try to focus despite the fact that his fingers are stroking my bare skin. "Remember when I told you about how I haven't been able to write sex scenes since I broke up with Sheldon?"

He nods. "Yes."

"And you told me that I'll be fine once I have sex with someone new. Well..." I pause, lifting my eyes to his. "Why not you? Maybe you'd want to be my guinea pig for this book." I chew my bottom lip, waiting for his response.

"You mean..."

I nod. "I want to get Sheldon cheating on me out of my head, and I need some new material to spice up my book. My last book didn't do so well, and I really want to knock this one out of the park. Plus, writing is always better when it comes from experience, and what better way to create steamy sex scenes than if I'm having it?"

He blinks. "So, you're saying that you want to have sex with me for research purposes...and then write about it in your book."

"Yep. That's pretty much it in a nutshell. We're both attracted to each other. Why not have fun with it while we're doing whatever it is that we're doing?" I play with the hem of my jersey. "What do you think?"

His eyes bounce between mine. "I'd be honored to let you use me as your sex muse."

A laugh bursts from my chest and I shove his shoulder. "Don't let it get to your head or anything."

"But I have one stipulation." He cups my face. "This isn't part of our agreement. You're running the show. We have sex when you say you want to have sex, and we stop when you want to stop. No contract, no time frame. Just you and me, enjoying each other."

"Deal." Excitement courses through my veins. "I have so many scenarios we can try out. I'll send you some links."

"Links?"

"You know, like, porn."

His eyes widen. "You watch porn?"

I hike a shoulder. "Don't you?"

"Sure, but you watch it for writing purposes?"

"Hell yeah. Not for the plot or anything, but for positions and stuff. Sometimes I need a little inspiration. My sex life hasn't been anything like the books I write."

A grin spreads across his face. "That's about to change."

12

TRENTON

This woman is going to be the death of me.

I pause the video she sent me and type out a response.

Me: You're killing me. It's only 2:00 and now I have to wait until tonight to see you.

Cassidy: I'm taking it you liked the video?

Me: Yeah, you could say that.

My dick hardens at the thought of seeing Cassidy above me, straddling my face while I make her come. The blonde in the video she sent me doesn't even come close to the way Cassidy would look with my head buried between her lush thighs.

Cassidy: I've always wanted to ride someone's face.

Me: No one's ever asked you to?

Cassidy: Nope. I'm a bit heavier than Sheldon. I think he was afraid of being suffocated to death.

Me: I can't think of a better way to go.
Me: And you're the perfect weight, so forget about that asshole.

THE THINGS I wanted to do to her last night with her ass in my hands, pinned against the door wearing *my* number...and when she told me she wanted to fuck me for inspiration for her book? I was ready to lie down at her feet and let her use me any way she wanted.

CASSIDY: Thanks for doing this for me.
Me: Any man would be crazy to turn you down.

I DIDN'T SEE any of this coming. Not the mini-feud we had when I first moved in; not the fake dating situation we ended up in; and certainly not the way my mind has been consumed with thoughts of her since she put sex on the table.

Cassidy Quinn has become my new addiction.

WE HAD our first away game tonight at Madison Square Garden, so it's late when I get back to New Jersey.

I should be exhausted, but adrenaline courses through my veins coming off tonight's win—and knowing what's about to happen once I step foot inside her apartment has my dick wide awake.

Cassidy opens the door wearing my jersey, and I have to restrain myself from pouncing on her.

"Hi." Her throat bobs as she steps back to let me inside.

I toss my bag onto the floor and close the door behind me. "Hi yourself."

"You played great tonight." She fidgets with the hem of the jersey, looking up at me from under her long dark lashes. "Another win."

I move toward her, slow like a lion stalking its prey. "You were watching?"

She nods, inching backward so I have to follow her. "Of course."

My eyes trail down her bare legs while my heart thunders in my chest. "Have you changed your mind about our agreement?"

She shakes her head. "Have you?"

"Not a chance."

Her feet stop, and mine close the distance between us until I'm able to reach out and tilt her face.

"I've been looking forward to this all day," she says, her breath dancing across my lips.

My thumb strokes her cheek. "I've been looking forward to making you come on my face."

My words are the shot at the starting line.

Cassidy pushes up onto her toes and slams her lips against mine. She claws at my shirt, pushing it up until I tear it over my head and drop it at our feet. In one quick swoop, I lift her into my arms and stalk into the bedroom.

I toss her onto the bed and the comforter puffs up around her. I couldn't tell you what color it is, or what the rest of her room looks like, because all I can focus on is the red lace peeking out from under the jersey she's wearing.

My eyebrows jump and she grins. "I know how much you liked these when you saw them in the laundry room."

"It's not the panties." I kneel over her and push the jersey up over her breasts to find the matching red lace clinging to her breasts. "It's the way they look on *you*. That's what I was thinking about that day—how fucking sexy you'd look in them."

She yanks the jersey over her head and tosses it onto the floor, lying back and letting me get the full visual. I commit every inch of her body to my memory; the way her nipples show through the material; the dips and curves of her soft belly; the way her thighs rub together to ease the ache I know is throbbing between them.

Cassidy flips onto her stomach and tosses me a devious glance over her shoulder.

"Goddamn." I reach out and grip two overflowing handfuls of her ass, loving the way the thin lace disappears between her cheeks. I lean down and sink my teeth into her ass before kissing my way up the small of her back. She shivers underneath me as I skim my hands along her ribs. I pop open the clasp on her bra and slide my hands around to cup her breasts, relishing in the way her hardened buds feel pressing against my palms.

I lower my lips to the cusp of her ear and press my dick against her ass so she can feel what she's doing to me. "You are perfect, Cassidy Quinn."

She moans and arches her back, twisting her neck so she can kiss me. I swear I could come just like this—my hands full with her tits, my cock grinding against her, and my tongue in her mouth.

But tonight isn't about me.

It's about giving this woman everything she wants.

I flip her over and toss her bra to the floor before sliding off her thong. My eyes don't know where to look first, eating up every inch of Cassidy's bare body. I dive down and suck one of her nipples into my mouth before switching to the other. I lap at her skin like a man starved, making my way down her stomach so I can kiss each stretch mark streaked across her hips.

Then I sit back on my heels and gaze down at her. Her cheeks are flushed, her chest is heaving, and her legs are spread wide.

She's like a fantasy come to life.

"Look at you." I slide my thumb over her pussy, swirling her arousal over her clit in slow circles. "Wet for me already. I bet you taste so good."

Her hips rock and she lets out a breathy moan. "Please, Trenton."

I move off the bed to stand, and pull off my pants and boxers.

Cassidy sits up on her elbows to watch me, her eyes following my hand as I pump my dick in slow strokes.

I tip my chin. "Get on your knees."

She does as I command, and for a moment I'm torn between wanting her to face me so I can gaze up at her tits as they bounce, and wanting her to face away from me so I can watch her ass move as she rides my face.

The latter wins.

I grip onto her hips, pulling her down until I can taste her on my lips. My tongue glides over her, and she lets out a loud moan.

I hum my approval. "Lower, Cassidy. Sit and let me worship you."

She widens her legs and gives me all of her weight, putting her pussy in my mouth. My nose is nestled between her ass cheeks and her arousal drips down my chin as I rub my tongue all over her.

Fuck, this is heaven.

"Keep touching yourself," she says. "I want to watch you make yourself come while I'm up here."

I wrap one hand around my dick and I groan against her pussy, feasting on her while I fuck my hand in ragged strokes.

Knowing she's watching me jerk off, knowing she's turned on by it, has me ready to explode.

Cassidy rolls her hips and reaches back to grab a fistful of my hair. "Oh God, Trent. Your tongue feels amazing."

Her sounds spur me on. The way she calls my name releases some primal animal inside me. I want to be the only name on her lips, the only name she screams—the only man making her feel this way.

Just one taste of her and I want Cassidy to be mine.

I come hard, unable to hold it together any longer.

Cassidy's moans grow louder, and her legs begin to shake. And when she comes, she smothers me and takes what she needs as she rides out her orgasm.

I'd gladly drown between these thighs.

Cassidy collapses onto the bed beside me while I reach over and pull a few tissues out of the box on her nightstand to clean off my stomach. Then I wrap her in my arms and she curls into me.

I think we're both in shock because it's a good few minutes before either of us speaks.

"That was..." Her voice trails off.

"So much hotter than the video."

"Exactly." She laughs against my chest. "That scene is definitely going into the book. The world needs to know about your tongue skills."

"I still can't believe you're writing scenes like this."

She rolls out of bed and runs into the living room before returning with one of her books. "Read this one. It's my favorite book I've ever written."

I arch a brow as I glance down at the cover. "*Say You'll Stay*. What's it about?"

"I'm not telling you. You have to go in blind. And I expect frequent progress updates."

I thumb through the pages. "I'm highly impressed that you're able to create an entire book like this."

She smiles. "You are?"

"Hell yeah. I could never do something like this." I set the book to the side and pull her body closer. "You're a very sexy woman, Cassidy Quinn. Brains and beauty."

She sighs. "Sounds like the total package to me."

"If only you could sing."

She swats at my chest and I hold her against me as she fights to get out of my grip. She tries to protest but I cut her off with a kiss, and she melts against my lips.

"You love my singing."

I bite her bottom lip. "For you, I'd lie and tell you I love your singing."

"Don't." She pulls back and looks into my eyes, the smile fading from her face. "Promise me. To the world, we can fake it, but don't lie to me."

"I promise I won't lie to you." I brush the tip of my nose against hers. "Promise you won't lie to me?"

"I promise."

I see sincerity in the depths of her hazel eyes, and the truth is, I believe her. I can't imagine a situation where Cassidy would lie to me about anything. She's genuine and real, and gives it to me straight.

But I've been deceived before, and I don't know if I'll ever be able to fully trust someone again.

I do know one thing for sure though: I can't wait for Cassidy to send me the next video.

13

CASSIDY

"DAMN, girl. This scene is fucking hot. Is it weird that I'm picturing you and Trent the whole time I'm reading it?"

"Only when you *tell me* you're picturing us." I grin. "It's good, isn't it? God, I've missed writing smut."

"Forget about writing it. You're *living* it." Aarya heaves a dramatic sigh. "I can't believe you're getting to live out your romance book fantasies with a professional hockey star."

My cheeks heat thinking about last night. "It is kind of crazy the way this is all happening."

"Have you checked outside your door yet?"

"No." I rub my temples in small circles. "I don't want to expect there to be flowers just because he left them once before."

"You're not expecting them. You're just *checking*."

"And what if they're not there and I feel disappointed because they're not there? What if I want there to be flowers there because I want him to *want* to get me flowers? But if there's no flowers, then that means he didn't want to get me flowers."

"You're confusing me. Just open the damn door."

I pull myself off the couch with a whine, and stomp over to the door. I hold my breath and count to three in my head before opening the door.

My mouth falls open.

"There're flowers, aren't there?"

"A giant bouquet of red roses." I crouch down and snatch the card.

Red is officially my new favorite color.
And you're my new favorite flavor.
—Neighbor Man

WETNESS POOLS BETWEEN MY LEGS. "Damn, this guy is good."

"He wrote you something freaky in his card, didn't he?"

I chuckle. "Maybe."

"Have you sent him any new videos?"

"Not yet. I don't want him to think I'm a crazy sex fiend or something."

"Well, I'm living vicariously through you so hurry up. I want the next chapter in this book."

"Why don't you come to the game with me tonight? Maybe you can find your own hockey star to bone."

She gasps. "Really? I can come with you?"

"Of course. I'll tell Celeste to get you a ticket."

Aarya squeals. "This is going to be so much fun."

"Let me give her a call now. We leave at six so make sure you're ready."

"Yes, ma'am. See you at six."

I shoot a text to Celeste, and then my thumb taps on Trenton's name.

ME: I love the flowers, but the note was my favorite part.

Trenton: I'm no author but I thought that was pretty clever.

Me: My best friend is coming with me to the game tonight.

Me: She requested that you hook her up with one of your teammates.

Trenton: Hmm. What kind of guys is she into?

Me: Just make sure he's nice. No assholes allowed.

Trenton: I'm on it.

Me: Is it too soon to send you another video?

Trenton: I was hoping you'd send one so I had another excuse to see you tonight.

SOMETHING FLUTTERS IN MY CHEST, but I stamp it down.

Of course he wants to see me. He's getting sexual favors for the sake of my writing. Like he said, any guy would be a willing participant.

This is a deal we've made.

Nothing more.

I scroll until I find the video I bookmarked and paste the link into the text.

ME: Here you go.

Me: And for the record, you don't need an excuse to see me.

Trenton: Good because I would've come up with one anyway.

"YES! GOAL!"

Aarya slaps her palms against mine. "This is so exciting! Who knew I was into hockey?"

I laugh at the intensity in her eyes. "It is exciting now that I know what's going on."

"I told you I'd make a hockey fan out of you." Celeste nudges me with her shoulder. "Trent has been in a great mood, by the way. I don't know what you're doing, but keep doing it."

Aarya stifles a laugh and I dig my elbow into her ribs.

I don't know if Trenton told Celeste about our agreement, but I don't feel comfortable telling many people about what we're doing.

The crowd is electric tonight. The score was 0-0, neither team giving up a goal until now.

The coach puts Trenton in for the final period, and excitement bubbles through my veins. He becomes a different person when he pulls down his mask and takes his position in the crease.

As soon as the puck drops, the center from Boston skates away with it, making a beeline for Trenton. He passes it to another player, but defense intercepts it. They fight for possession by the net.

"Come on, get the puck out of there!" Celeste shouts.

Then one of the Boston players shoulder-checks Trenton's teammate, sending him flying backward—right into Trenton. His helmet flies off as he slides across the ice and a fight breaks out around him. Gloves come off and several of the players fall on top of Trenton. Fists fly and the crowd goes wild until the ref finally stops it. Trenton's teammate helps him up, and I crane my neck to see if he's okay.

Celeste leans over to explain to Aarya. "You're not allowed to touch the goalie. It's no holds barred."

Aarya's wide eyes flick between us. "That was nuts."

This was the first live fight I've seen. The idea of fighting on ice where sharp blades are involved makes me worry for Trenton's safety. I stare at him, unable to focus on anything else until he turns around and searches for me. We lock eyes and he gives me a quick nod before slamming the helmet back over his head.

Celeste puts her arm around my waist. "He's okay, babe. Just a little scuffle."

My lips pull into a frown. "Why can't they just play the damn game? Why do they have to fight like that? It's not safe."

"Because it's hot as fuck," Aarya says.

Celeste laughs. "His team had his back. They won't let him get hurt."

The fight sparked a fire underneath the Goldfinches and they secure a win minutes before the end of the period, making the final score 2-0.

I pace in my living room waiting for Trenton to get back after the game. Something feels different tonight. Maybe it's the fact that I saw him go down on the ice, or maybe it's just nerves because I'm excited to see him.

But I won't be able to relax until he comes home.

I fling open the door when I hear his knock and jump into his arms.

He chuckles as he staggers backward, wrapping his arms around me. "Hello to you too."

"Are you okay? Let me see your head." I grip his face and examine his face. "Do you need to go to the hospital?"

Trenton walks into my apartment and kicks the door shut behind him. "I'm fine."

"I was worried. Your helmet came off. You could've gotten seriously hurt."

"Listen to me." He carries me over to the couch and lowers me onto his lap so I'm straddling him as he sits. "We get hurt in hockey. It's a physical sport. But I'm always going to be okay."

I frown. "I didn't like it."

A slow smile spreads across his face before he brushes his nose against mine. "You were worried about me, baby?"

"Of course I was worried."

"Come to think of it, I'm in a bit of pain right now." His hands slide down my back and grip my ass, dragging me over his growing bulge. "You think you can make me feel better?"

I rock my hips, my fingers threading through his hair. "I can make you feel amazing."

The video I sent Trenton was more about me giving than receiving this time. After watching him jerk off last night, I wanted to be the one to give him pleasure. I want to be the one to make him come, to be the reason he loses control.

I slide off his lap and lead him to my bedroom. Then I begin undressing him, taking my time to peel off each article of clothing until he's left standing in his boxers.

I kneel in front of him, wearing his jersey and nothing else, and gaze up at him. "I want to do this exactly like the video. If it's too much, I'll pull back, but don't be afraid of hurting me."

He nods, his eyes wild with desire.

I pull his jersey over my head and discard it on the floor before reaching for his boxers, dragging it down his muscular legs. His dick bobs before me, a shiny glint of precum beading at his head. He's thick and long, and my pussy clenches at the sight of him.

I slide my lips around him, sucking his crown into my mouth and bobbing in slow, short pulses.

Trenton's hands push through my hair as he lets out a groan.

I run my fingernails up his thighs and reach around to grip his ass, pushing him farther into my mouth. I hum as I take him all the way in before pulling back and doing it again.

My eyes flick up to his, letting him know want I want.

His grip on my hair tightens as he thrusts his hips, plunging deeper to the back of my throat. I gag and he pulls back for only a moment before he shoves himself back inside.

He's holding my head still while he fucks my face, my eyes watering as his cock hits the back of my throat—and I've never been so turned on in my life.

"Fuck, baby. You look so good gagging on my cock. What a good girl you are."

Wetness drips down my thigh as Trenton talks me through it, praising me and letting me know how much he's enjoying this. I slide my fingers over my pussy, trying to relieve some of the mounting pressure.

"Don't you come, baby. Not yet. I want to be the one to do it."

I whimper in protest, but then his hips move faster. I reach up to cup his balls, giving them a gentle tug.

He groans loud. "Cassidy, I'm gonna come."

And this big, beautiful man calls my name, over and over again, as he shoots his release down my throat. I swallow it down and my chest heaves as I try to catch my breath. But then I'm yanked up by my shoulders and Trenton hauls my mouth against his, suffocating me in a kiss.

He carries me to the bed and tosses me onto it before burying his face between my legs. He laps up my arousal and sucks on my clit, feasting on me as if he needs me like the air he breathes. It's messy and wet and loud—his grunts and my moans, the both of us enjoying this just as much as the other.

It doesn't take long for me to break apart, my body at his mercy. I clamp my thighs around his head and ride out the intense euphoria.

When we're both sated, he collapses onto the bed next to me and pulls me into him. Our panting breaths mingle as I lay my head on his chest. His heartbeat races, matching the pace of my own. We don't speak for a long while, and I'm not sure what he's thinking...but I recognize the sound of warning bells going off in my head.

I could get used to this.

I like the way this feels. The way *he* feels—here, holding me. The flowers, the notes, the kissing, the sex...I like it all too much. None of this was supposed to happen, but now that it has, I don't want it to stop.

It has to stop at some point, right?

What if it doesn't?

What if this is just the start of something incredible?

I guess I'll find out.

All I know is, with the way he's making me come, I'll ride this train until the wheels fall off.

14

TRENTON

"HEY, Warden. What are you reading over there?"

I glance two rows ahead of me. "My girl's book."

McKinley waggles his eyebrows. "I heard your girl writes porn."

"We watch it; women read it. It's all the same in the end."

Krumkachova turns around in his seat to join the conversation. "What's that one about?"

I stick my bookmark inside and turn the cover to face them. "A woman gets into a car accident and wakes up two weeks later, not knowing who pulled her out of the wreck. She has amnesia and can't remember anything about her life before the accident, including her boyfriend."

"Damn, that sucks." McKinley smacks Stamos on the shoulder. "Imagine your wife waking up and not remembering who you are?"

Stamos grunts. "I'd make her fall in love with me all over again."

"Or I'd sneak in and convince her to be with me instead."

Stamos punches him in the arm. "You fucking wish."

McKinley returns his attention to me. "Is her writing any good?"

"Fuck yeah, it's good." Pride swells in my chest. "I haven't been able to put this book down."

I've never really been much of a reader. I read for school when I had to, but books haven't been able to hold my attention as an adult. I don't know if it's because I know Cassidy wrote this, or if it's just that good, but I'm into this story.

"Writing is her passion. She was having a bit of writer's block since her ex cheated on her, but lately she's found her groove again and she's working on a new book."

"Yeah, I bet she found her groove." McKinley shoots me a wink. "You showed her who the warden of that pussy is."

We all groan and Stamos slams his fist into his shoulder.

"Ow, would you stop hitting me?"

"Then stop saying stupid shit."

"I want to read a sex scene." McKinley reaches across the aisle and holds out his hand. "Let me see."

I flip to the last intimate scene I read, and pass the book to him. I watch as his eyes skim over the page, his eyebrows jumping every now and again.

"Shit, your girl is freaky, Warden."

"Mac, read it out loud," Krumkachova calls out.

McKinley clears his throat. "*Get on the bed and let me look at you.* I do as he commands and he hums his approval. *This pussy is mine, do you hear me?* I nod, and he slips a finger inside me while his thumb draws idle circles around my clit. My hips rock against his hand, chasing the orgasm I so desperately need. *You're so wet,* he whispers in my ear. *But I'm not going to let you come on my fingers.* He slips out of me and coats his cock in my arousal, pumping himself in hard strokes. *I want you to come all over my cock as you scream my name. Understand?* I nod as I whimper, unable to form words because of how turned on I am." McKinley's eyes flick to mine as he lets the book drop into his lap. "Well, now I have a boner."

Stamos punches his arm again. "Get the fuck away from me."

"Hell, no. I have to see how this scene ends. I'm invested now."

The bus is pin drop silent as McKinley continues reading, not one of us lifting our eyes to look at each other.

After the chapter ends, McKinley passes me the book and turns around to sit back against his seat.

Stamos howls with laughter. "Holy shit, Warden. Your girl just rendered Mac speechless. Hell must be freezing over."

"Fuck you." McKinley adjusts the seat of his pants. "That shit was hot."

Stamos turns back to me. "I'd read one of Cassidy's books. My wife is always telling me about the books she reads."

"We should start a book club," Krumkachova says. "We're always bored when we're on the road."

My eyebrows hit my hairline. "That's a great idea. She'd love that."

"When Stams' wife started her catering business, we hired her for all our events. And when Sully's girl was making handbags, we got her name out there too." Krumkachova lifts his chin. "Our family sticks together."

Family. The word leaves a bad taste in my mouth. I thought my old team was my family. I thought we were going to be friends for the rest of our lives. Look how that turned out.

"Hey." Krumkachova locks his dark eyes with mine. "We're family now. None of that bullshit with your old team happens with us. You got me?"

I give him a tight nod. My doubt must've been written all over my face. He's right though. What happened back in Seattle really sucked, but that's not how most friends operate. Just because Petroski betrayed my friendship doesn't mean these guys will.

My mind wanders to Cassidy.

Maybe the same can be said for her.

I slip my phone out of my pocket and type out a text to her.

Me: You just gave my entire team a boner.

Cassidy: What?!

Me: Mac just read one of your sex scenes out loud on the bus.

Cassidy: Why is he reading my book?

Me: They asked what I was reading. I showed them.

Me: They want to read your books now. I think you have a whole new fanbase.

Cassidy: That would be epic. Hockey players reading romance books.

Me: I'm thinking we could hook up Aarya with Krumkachova.

Cassidy: Oooo yes. The quiet broody ones are always hot.

Me: You sure you don't want me to set him up with you?

Cassidy: Do you think he'd be into me?

Me: Watch it, Quinn.

Cassidy: Or what?

Me: Or I'm going to have to teach you a lesson and remind you who you belong to.

Cassidy: I might like that.

Me: You would.

Me: For the record, you can't have any of my teammates.

Cassidy: For the record, I don't want any of them.

Cassidy: Your ex was a fool for letting you go.

WARMTH SEEPS INTO MY CHEST, spreading out to my arms and legs, blanketing me in comfort.

I tap out one last text before putting my phone back in my pocket.

ME: I miss you.

AFTER SECURING A WIN AGAINST BOSTON, the team is like a herd of pent-up bulls in Krumkachova's hotel room.

McKinley whines. "But we won. It's not fair that we don't get to celebrate."

"You know what this town is like after they lose." Stamos passes him a shot glass. "We can't risk getting into any trouble."

Krumkachova nods in agreement. "We'll celebrate once we get back. Our city will be waiting for us."

When each of us holds a glass of Fireball, we clink them together and toss them back.

I grimace as the liquid burns my throat. "Fuck, I hate shots."

"That's because you're an old man," McKinley says.

I glare at him. "Just wait until you're the veteran on the team, and you have some prick without a Stanley Cup under his belt calling you old."

Stamos and Krumkachova howl.

"Oh, shit." McKinley claps his hands. "That was good. You got me there. I bow down to the king."

"Man, that game was epic." Stamos shakes his head as he recalls my championship win. "I watched Panettiere shoot that biscuit at you and I swore it was going in, but you stopped it. Never seen a save like that before."

Krumkachova grunts. "Your reaction time is quick as fuck."

I glance down at the empty shot glass, not sure how to handle the unexpected praise from my teammates. "Winning the cup was a dream I've had since I was a kid. I'm just glad my mother was still around to see it happen."

Even if it was from a hospital bed.

"Good for you, man." Krumkachova pats my shoulder. "Not all of us are that lucky. I lost my mom a couple of years ago."

"Fuck, enough of this morbid bullshit." McKinley pours himself another shot. "What's your drink of choice, Warden?"

"I just like a cold beer after a game."

"I can get behind that." Stamos rises from the bed and digs into the fully-stocked mini-fridge, pulling out two bottles. "Hope you don't mind Corona."

"I'll take whatever you got. Thanks."

We talk about tonight's game, and one beer turns into two.

Then my phone buzzes in my pocket.

. . .

Cassidy: I was going to send you another video, but then I thought...

Cassidy: Why not make my own video instead.

A VIDEO COMES THROUGH, and I make sure to turn down my volume before clicking play.

Cassidy's legs fill the screen as she situates the camera at a particular angle. It looks like she's in bed, and it takes a moment for me to register what she's doing.

Until her hand slips underneath her black panties and I realize what's happening.

Holy fucking shit.

I pause the video and lock my screen, facing it down on my leg. My eyes dart around the room, but the guys are in the middle of a heated debate about beer brands. I lift the phone and type out a quick text.

Me: Are you trying to kill me, woman?

Cassidy: I'm waiting for you to call me, but I won't wait all night.

Cassidy: I can only tease myself for so long.

Me: Give me five minutes.

I SLIP my phone into my pocket and stand with my empty beer bottle in my hand.

"I'm going to call it a night, guys."

McKinley protests like I knew he would. "Already? But it's early. Come on, old man."

Stamos smirks like he knows my secret. "Your girl just texted you, didn't she?"

I fight to hide my grin. "I don't know what you're talking about."

Krumkachova shakes his head, but he's smiling. "Go have fun."

McKinley's head whips around. "Wait, what's going on? Why are you all speaking in code?"

I shoot him a wink. "That's the good thing about being older: You're wiser too."

The guys hoot and holler as I dart out of the room. I all but break into a full sprint down the hallway.

As soon as I lock the door behind me, I press Cassidy's name to FaceTime her.

Her beautiful face fills the screen and I can only make out her bare shoulders and collar bone in the frame, her hair fanned out on her pillow. "That was fast."

"Had to get to my girl."

She lets out a small moan. "I miss you."

I kick out of my sneakers and yank off my pants, leaving them at the foot of the bed. "God, I miss you. I wish I could be there right now."

She flips the camera to show me what she's doing. Her panties are pushed down around her knees and her fingers slide over her clit as her hips rock in a slow rhythm.

I prop myself against the headboard of the bed and free myself from my boxers to join Cassidy as she touches herself.

"I'm imagining you're here," she says. "Touching me. Sliding your fingers over me. Making me feel good."

I groan as I fist my cock. "I'd make you feel so good. Show me how wet you are."

She lifts her fingers, and they glisten in the dim lighting of her bedroom. "Are you hard, Trent?"

"Of course, I am." I flip my camera. "Look at what you do to me, baby."

She moans again. "I can't wait to feel your cock inside me. I want to fuck you when you get back."

"How do you want it, Cassidy? Do you want me on top, fucking you into the mattress, pinning your wrists above your head with your legs pressed up into your chest? Or do you want to ride me and bounce on my cock so I can watch those pretty tits move?" I pump myself in quick strokes, the thought alone bringing me closer to my release. "Or maybe you want me to fuck you from behind so I can spank your ass while I watch your pussy swallow me whole."

"Oh god, Trent. All of it. I want all of it." Cassidy's fingers move faster as her knees fall open. "I just want it with you."

Possession rips through me. "I'll give you anything you want, Cassidy. You're mine, and I'm going to make you feel so good."

"Yes, Trent. Yours."

Cassidy cries out, and I let go so we can come together. I watch as the orgasm rolls through her body, wishing I could be there to feel her, to taste her, to hear her panting in my ear.

She sighs as she relaxes, rolling onto her side and flipping the camera back to her face.

I grin. "I love the way you look after you come."

Hair a mess, flushed cheeks, a sated smile.

Until she pouts. "You're not here for post-orgasm snuggles."

"I'll make it up to you tomorrow, beautiful."

Tomorrow can't come fast enough.

15

TRENTON

MY HEART POUNDS a furious rhythm against my chest as I lift my knuckles to Cassidy's door.

The five-hour drive from Boston felt like an eternity knowing what was waiting for me back home.

Rather, *who* was waiting for me.

But when Cassidy swings open her door, my heart stops altogether.

She barely lifts her red-rimmed eyes to mine. "Hey, Trent."

"What's wrong?" I rush inside her apartment and drop my bags, clutching her face in my hands. "What happened? Why are you crying?"

She sniffles. "Candy died."

Fuck. I wrap my arms around her in a bear hug. "Cass, I'm so sorry."

Her muffled words come out in clips against my chest. "This morning...I didn't hear her...she wasn't chirping...I found her...on the bottom of the cage."

Sadness slices through my heart like a sharp knife. "Do you think she was sick?"

"I don't know." She slips her arms around my waist and fists my shirt. "I didn't notice anything."

I grip her tighter. "It's okay, baby. I've got you. I'm here now. Let it all out."

Sobs rack her body, the sound of her grief cracking my chest wide open. She loved that bird, and though I wasn't a fan of Candy, she was a living thing and now she's gone.

I lift her in my arms, cradling her as I carry her over to the couch. "I'm so sorry, my sweet girl."

She buries her face in my neck, her tears rolling down my skin as they fall. "She was like my best friend. She was such a good listener."

"She was. And she put up with your God-awful singing."

Cassidy hiccups as she laugh-sobs. "She liked my singing."

I stroke the back of her head, running my fingers through her soft hair. My chest physically aches me hearing her cry, seeing her upset like this.

In this moment, it hits me: I'll do anything to keep Cassidy safe and happy.

She's kind and caring and innocent, and I'll stop at nothing to make sure that no harm comes to her. I'll protect her from anything and anyone who tries to hurt her.

I don't ever want to see her cry like this again.

"I wasn't able to..." Cassidy pulls back and glances at the cage in the corner of the room. "She's still in there. I couldn't do it."

"It's okay, baby. I'll take care of it for you. Do you want to bury her somewhere, or get her cremated?"

"I think I'd like to bury her." She wipes her nose with the back of her hand. "Maybe by the tree I found her nest near when I rescued her and her brother."

My head tilts. "Candy had a brother?"

She nods. "She pecked him to death."

I can't help my reaction. "She *what?*"

"I rescued them and wanted to keep them together because they were family, you know? But apparently, they weren't supposed to live confined in the same cage. One day, I came home and found her brother on the bottom of the cage, blood and feathers everywhere. She pecked him to death."

Jesus Christ. Well, now her name makes perfect sense.

"I don't know what's more terrifying—Candy bludgeoning her brother to death, or you finding it funny to name her after an axe murderer."

"Trent," she whines.

"I'm sorry, I'm sorry." I wrap my arms around her shoulders to comfort her again. "But damn."

She lets out a soft laugh and rests her head on my shoulder. "I'm sorry about all the crying. I know this wasn't what you expected when you came over today. We can have sex in a little while."

My body stills and then I hold her away from me so I can look into her eyes. "We're *not* having sex, and that is the furthest thing from my mind right now. You're upset."

"I know, but we said we would do it when you got home and I don't want to disappoint you." She hikes a shoulder. "It's part of our deal."

I stare at her in disbelief. "Cassidy, nothing you say or do could disappoint me unless you said you didn't want to talk to me ever again. I'm not here because I want to fuck you. That's not what this is."

"It's not?"

"No." My throat bobs as I swallow. "I'm here because...because I want to see you. Because I need to be near you. Because I missed you while I was gone, and all I could think about when I wasn't playing hockey was you." My eyes bounce between hers. "We only have sex if you're in the mood to have sex. And if you're not, that doesn't mean I don't want to spend time with you."

A lone tear trails over the curve of her cheekbone, but I know this one isn't because of her bird.

"You're more than just sex, Cassidy Quinn. You're the total package, remember?"

She leans forward and presses her soft lips to mine. "I really missed you."

I really fucking did too.

"I HAVE A FEELING this is going to end badly."

"No, it won't. You've got this. I believe in you." I adjust the helmet on Cassidy's head and clip it under her chin. "There."

"I look ridiculous."

I bite my bottom lip to keep from freeing my smile. "You look safe."

She does look ridiculous but it's the most adorable kind. Elbow pads and knee pads wrap around her joints, and a bright-pink helmet protects her head. Her bottom lip sticks out at she pouts and I'm tempted to suck on it.

I hold up the rollerblades I bought her this afternoon. "Let's put on the finishing touches."

She groans as she lowers herself onto the curb. "You promise this is legal, right? I can't go to jail. I'd get eaten alive."

I kneel down and take her ankle into my hand as I slip her foot into the skate. "It's totally legal. I would never let anything bad happen to you."

Since the nineties, Manhattan has been hosting Wednesday Night Skate—an event where skaters of all experience levels can come together and skate along a ten-mile route through the city's most popular spots. I used to participate when I visited my grandmother each summer, until college and hockey took over. When Cassidy told me she'd never skated before, I knew I had to bring her here.

Once her skates are laced up, I stand and hold out my hands. She slaps her palms against mine and her legs wobble as she rises from the sidewalk, but I steady her.

"I've got you. You're good. Now, eyes on me."

Cassidy's eyes flick to mine.

"There she is." I smile and squeeze her hands. "We're going to take this nice and slow."

She arches a brow. "Is it me, or are you making this really sexual?"

"You're a horn dog, so everything sounds sexual to you."

"I can't help it. Look at you." Her gaze roams over me. "Even in rollerblades and a helmet, I'd still hit it."

I bark out a laugh. "Stop trying to distract me. I'm teaching you how to skate whether you like it or not."

I tug on Cassidy's arms, and skate backwards while I pull her along a side street. Her legs jerk as she tries to maintain balance, but after a few minutes, her body relaxes.

"This isn't so bad," she says.

"See? Now, I want you to alternate your legs and push off the ground, propelling yourself forward."

"Don't let me go."

"I won't. Hold onto me and try skating yourself."

Her body stiffens as she figures out how to move her legs in fluid strides.

"Good, now you'll let go of one of my hands."

She grimaces. "Wait, I'm not ready."

"You can do it, Cassidy."

She drops my right hand, and I swivel around to the side so it looks like we're holding hands while we skate.

Her eyes light up. "I'm doing it!"

"Yes, you are. Move your free arm with you as you skate and let your body fall into a rhythm. Side to side."

We glide up and down the block until Cassidy feels comfortable enough to skate on her own.

She squeals. "It's happening. I'm skating."

I laugh at how excited she is to do something she should've done when she was a kid. It saddens me to think of little spunky Cassidy with parents who didn't take care of her, or spend time with her, or love her.

After I teach her how to turn and stop, it's time to head to Union Square. The skate takes place at midnight, but everyone gathers about fifteen minutes beforehand.

"Wow, there are a lot of people here." Cassidy's eyes scan the area. "I've never seen anything like this before."

I squeeze her hand. "I've never done this with anyone before."

She gazes up at me from under her long dark lashes. "No?"

I tilt her helmet and dip my head to press my lips against her. "Just you."

She wraps her hands around the back of my neck. "Thank you for cheering me up tonight. I really needed to get out of the house."

"Of course." I slide my hands into her back pockets. "I don't like seeing you sad."

Her cheeks tinge a pretty pink color. "It's nice being out here without all the paparazzi. It's like we're a real, normal couple."

Real. As if we aren't. As if what we're doing here tonight is part of the PR stunt.

Is that all this is to Cassidy? Is it the reason she's with me tonight, because she thinks it's part of our agreement? Does she feel obligated to spend time with me?

"Trenton Ward."

My head jerks up in the direction of the man calling my name. Then a smile spreads across my face. "Hey, Mannie."

He skids to a stop in front of us and claps me on the back. "Long time no see. How the hell are you?"

"I'm great. How have you been?"

"I'm fantastic. You know me." He looks to Cassidy and sticks out his hand. "I'm Emanuel. You can call me Mannie. Everyone else here does."

She shakes his hand. "It's nice to meet you, Mannie. I'm Cassidy."

"Oh, I know who you are." He winks. "You two have been the talk of the tri-state area over the last few weeks."

I shake my head. "Still reading the tabloids?"

"My husband loves them. I pretend to hate them, but I secretly love hearing about all the celebrity gossip."

Cassidy laughs. "Is he here too?"

"My husband would die before he let me put him in a pair of skates. I'm here with our daughter." He glances at the crowd. "She's around here somewhere."

I wrap my arm around Cassidy's shoulders. "This is her first time here."

"First time skating too," she adds.

"Well, you're in very good hands," he says.

"Would you mind taking a picture of us, Mannie?" Cassidy

unzips her crossbody bag and hands him her phone before wrapping her arms around my waist.

I lean down and press my cheek against hers, engulfing her in my arms. Mannie snaps a few photos, and then I smack my lips against her cheek, squishing her face while she laughs.

"They came out great." Mannie hands Cassidy her phone and gives her a quick hug. "It was wonderful to meet you. Enjoy your night."

Then he sets his hand on my shoulder. "Cherish each other."

I nod. "We will."

Cassidy's eyebrows lift after Mannie skates away. "What was that about?"

"He lost his boyfriend about ten years ago. Drunk driver hit him here in the city. Now he's all about appreciating the moment you're in and cherishing the people you have in your life."

Her lips tug into a frown. "That's so sad."

"It is." I watch the back of his head as he skates farther into the crowd. "But he found love again, and he's happy. He has a family."

"Do you want a family someday, Trenton Ward?"

"I do." I glance down at Cassidy. "What about you?"

"I think I'd like to be a mom."

I can picture it. Cassidy in a skin-tight dress with her swollen belly sticking out of it, looking hot as hell.

Then my mind fabricates an image of Cassidy at a hockey game holding our son or daughter, wearing a mini-jersey. It's black and yellow with a small goldfinch on the front, and my name on the back.

What the fuck is wrong with me?

Why am I imagining Cassidy having my child?

And why am I getting hard at the thought of spilling my cum inside her?

Cassidy places her hand on my forearm. "You okay?"

No, I'm not okay.

Not one fucking bit.

"SKATING through the tunnel was the coolest thing I've ever done."

I stop beside Cassidy's door and lean against the wall. "I'm glad you had fun."

"It was so fun. I want to do it again one day."

"Then we will."

She glances at the door and pauses. "Candy won't be there when I go inside."

I brush my thumb against her cheek. "No, she won't."

She frowns, and I hate it so much.

She digs into her purse for her key card, but I cover her hand with mine to stop her. "Stay with me tonight."

Her eyes fly to mine. "You don't have to do that. I'm a big girl. I'll be fine."

I wrap her in my arms and speak against her lips as I pull her close. "Does being a big girl mean you can't snuggle with your boyfriend?"

"I don't know the rules for fake boyfriends. Are snuggles in the contract?"

She's teasing me, I know, but my heart sinks at her reminder.

"Snuggles are in the fine print." I pepper kisses all over her face. "Come on. Stay with me tonight."

She sighs against my mouth. "Okay. But if you snore, I'm punching you in the throat."

"So violent."

"You like it."

"I do."

There isn't anything about this woman I don't like.

16

CASSIDY

Waking up in Trenton's bed is like waking up in a five-star resort.

Waking up with his arms around me isn't half-bad either.

"It feels like I'm sleeping on a cloud. A big, fluffy cloud, floating through the sky."

Trenton's laugh is raspy with the sound of the morning still wrapped around his throat. "I'm glad you like it. It's one of the only things I splurged on in this place."

"Worth it." I scoot back to get closer to him, relishing in the warmth of his massive body surrounding me. "Can we stay here all day?"

"I wish." He groans as he presses his erection against me. "I have a press conference this morning, and then I'm going to meet Toby and his mother at his school."

"He's going to be so excited to meet you." I reach back and grip his hair while he bites my neck. "Find out who his bullies are and shove them in a trash can."

He chuckles as his hand snakes around to cup my breast. "I don't think that'd go over too well for me in the media."

"No, probably not." I drag his hand down my stomach and slip it under my panties. "How much time do we have?"

"Enough time to make you come."

"WATCH THIS."

I click send, and wait for Trenton to open his phone. Aarya and I watch from the bar as he pulls out his phone from his pocket.

He looks damn good tonight, with the sleeves of his black shirt rolled up on his forearms.

"Look at the way he smiles when he sees your name on the screen." Aarya nudges me. "That boy is smitten."

"He's not smitten. He's horny."

"Right. Keep telling yourself that."

As soon as Trenton opens the link I sent him, his eyebrows jump and he turns his phone away from his friends sitting next to him. Then his thumbs fly across the screen before a text pops up on my phone.

TRENTON: I'm convinced you live to torture me.

Me: *angel emoji*

Trenton: You're an angel who looks like sin.

Me: That was a good line. I think I'll add that to my book.

Trenton: When do I get to read this book?

Me: When it's done.

Me: We still have some more scenes to recreate. What do you think of the video?

Trenton: I'm in.

Me: You didn't even watch the whole thing.

Trenton: Doesn't matter. If it involves seeing you naked, then I'm in.

"WHO'S the guy who just walked in and sat down next to Trent?"

I glance up from my phone. "That's Alexander Krumkachova. They call him Krum Cake."

"I call him sex on a stick."

I chuckle and slip my phone back into my purse. "Come on. Let's go say hi. I haven't met him yet."

Aarya and I take our drinks and walk back to the boys' table. They have their own VIP section upstairs overlooking the dance floor below.

Trenton stands and wraps his arm around my waist. "This is Cassidy, and her friend Aarya."

Krumkachova pushes to his feet and shakes my hand. "It's nice to finally meet you. I'm halfway through your book. It's excellent."

My eyes widen. "You're reading *Say You'll Stay* too?"

Trenton squeezes my hip. "All the guys are."

I dig my elbow into Aarya's ribs. "Would you look at that? Professional hockey players are reading my book, yet my own best friend hasn't."

She scoffs. "I've read your sex scenes."

"Not the same thing."

Krumkachova's head tilts. "Why haven't you read her books?"

Aarya shrugs. "I'm not into reading. And I can't stand that Hallmark channel romance bullshit."

His eyes narrow. "You think love is bullshit?"

"I didn't say love is bullshit. I just don't buy into all that romantic crap. It sets these unrealistic expectations for women. No guy is going to do the things you read in a book. It's damaging for a young girl to read that and assume a man is going to come along and sweep her off her feet."

He crosses his arms over his chest. "Men can be romantic."

She laughs. "I've never met a man who has done any of those things."

"Then you haven't been spending time with the right men."

"There are billions of people in the world—there's no way that there's one end-all-be-all for each of us."

McKinley joins us and slaps Trenton on the back. "Come on. You can't tell me there's no such thing as love. Just look at these two love birds. They're fucking adorable."

My cheeks heat as I look up at Trenton. "What do you think,

Neighbor Man? Do you believe in soulmates and the *romantic bullshit* I write?"

"I believe in love." His dark eyes meet mine and hold my gaze for a moment before he answers. "I believe in caring about someone so much that you'd do anything for them. I believe in putting someone's happiness over your own. I believe in showing them every single day how much they mean to you, even if it's in little ways to let them know you're thinking of them. So, whether romance means flowers and jewelry, or taking a lavish trip to Greece, or simply showing up when they need you, I think the right person will do those things for you when he loves you. And if it's real, no one and nothing could take that love away."

My lungs constrict and suddenly I'm struggling to breathe.

Krumkachova leans in and points to Trenton. "The way he's looking at her?" He turns his attention to Aarya. "*That* isn't fake romance bullshit. *That* is real love."

Aarya locks eyes with me, and disappointment seeps into my chest. We both know the truth: Trenton doesn't love me. We're just pretending.

Why does that hurt so much?

"Come on." Aarya grabs my elbow. "Let's go dance."

I'm thankful for the distraction from the heavy conversation, and shake it off as we head into the middle of the dance floor.

"You okay?" Aarya asks.

"Yeah, that was just..."

"Intense?"

I laugh and roll my eyes. "Exactly."

"I don't know, Cass. From where I was standing, Trent looked sincere. I think you two need to have a conversation."

"He was just faking it. I will not be the one who catches feelings in this scenario."

"Not even if he catches feelings too?"

I squeeze my eyes shut and shake my head. "I don't know. I don't want to talk about this anymore. Let's just have fun tonight."

She lifts her arms above her head and shakes her hips from side to side. "Got it, boss."

We dance until my feet are numb and the hair on the back of my neck is damp. It feels good to let loose and forget about everything for a while.

But then two strong arms wrap around my waist, and *that* feels good too.

Trenton's familiar scent surrounds me, and his warm breath hits the cusp of my ear. "I'm having a hard time focusing on anything other than you in this dress tonight."

I grin, rolling my hips and pushing myself against him. "That was the point of wearing it."

I went shopping this weekend and found an olive-green backless halter dress at my favorite boutique. The rouching on the sides accentuates my ass, and I knew Trenton would love the easy access to my breasts.

It feels like every thought I have lately revolves around him. It's more than the porn I send him. I bought this dress because I wanted to drive him crazy. I surprised him with a BBQ pork sandwich from Hamilton's after practice the other day because I knew he'd be hungry. I even found another skating event in New Jersey to send him so we can check it out together.

I'm acting like this relationship is real, like he's my real boyfriend.

The lines are getting so blurred, and there's no one to blame but myself. I'm the one who suggested getting sexual. We wouldn't be this close, this intimate, if it weren't for me.

Yet the thought of pumping the breaks now makes my insides twist. I don't want to stop what we're doing. I don't want to change a thing.

I just worry about what's going to happen to my heart when this is all over.

Trenton's fingers skim my ribs, sending goosebumps flying along my skin as he inches further, and the worries weighing on my mind dissipate in an instant.

"Tell me, baby," he whispers. "If I slipped my fingers inside your dress, would your nipples be hard?"

I glance at Aarya, but she's busy dancing with Krumkachova.

I lift my arms and wrap them around the back of Trenton's neck, leaning my head back against his chest. "Why don't you see for yourself?"

His hand slides in through the side of my dress, and his fingertips graze my hardened peak. I bite my bottom lip to keep from moaning, though I doubt anyone would hear me above the pounding bass.

"I want to take you right here." He nips at my neck. "Think anyone would notice?"

I smile and twist around to greet his lips. "Think anyone would notice if we just left?"

Without another word, Trenton pulls me through the crowded room, weaving through people until we get to the exit.

Excitement courses through me as we step outside and the cool night air hits my sweaty skin. Trenton holds the phone to his ear, calling the team's driver who's on standby around the corner, and clutches me tight with his other hand.

But a flash goes off in front of us, startling me, and all I see are spots.

"Trenton!"

"Cassidy!"

A frenzy of shouting people surrounds us, snapping pictures so fast, it looks like a strobe light.

Trenton sticks his phone back in his pocket and tugs on my arm. "Come on, this way."

We barrel through the crowd, Trenton pushing people out of his way to clear a path. The paparazzi shove their cameras in our faces, disregarding personal space or safety.

Then a man grabs my arm, yanking me away from Trenton. I trip over someone's foot and tumble to the ground, smashing my knee onto the sidewalk. I shield my head with both arms, praying no one stomps on me.

"Get the fuck away from her," I make out Trenton's voice above the commotion. "Back the fuck up."

I'm pulled off the ground and panic seizes me until I see Trenton's face. "It's me, baby. It's me. I've got you."

I grip onto his shoulders, burying my face in his neck to hide from the cameras, and I don't look up until we're safely in the car.

"Are you okay?" Trenton grips my face, his eyes bouncing between mine, wide with worry. "I'm so sorry I couldn't get you out of there sooner. Does your knee hurt bad?"

I glance down. "Oh, shit."

My knee is already swelling, the skin around the cut turning a light-purple, and blood trickles down my shin.

"I tripped. I couldn't see where I was going."

"Do you want me to go to the hospital?" the driver says, eyeing me in the rear-view mirror.

"No," I say, at the same time Trenton says, "Yes."

I shake my head. "It's just a bruised knee. It's not broken or anything."

"We should get it checked out." Trenton cradles my calf. "Can you move it?"

I grit my teeth while I bend my leg, moving it up and down. "I'll put some ice on it when we get back to the apartment."

"Cassidy—"

"Please, Trent. That was a lot back there. I just want to go home and relax."

"Fine." He blows out a frustrated breath through his nose like a bull. "Please take us home, Sam."

Sam nods and flips on his blinker.

Ten minutes later, after Trenton insists on carrying me into the building, holding me the entire elevator ride up to the sixth floor, and down the long stretch of the hallway until we're inside my apartment.

I kick off my shoes while Trenton grabs the bag of frozen corn in my freezer. I collapse onto the couch and he pulls my legs onto his lap while he carefully sets the bag on my knee.

I hiss. "That's cold."

He shakes his head, staring down at my legs as he caresses them. "I'm so sorry, Cassidy. This is my fault. I should've had Sam waiting for us. I should've gone out the VIP exit. I wasn't thinking straight. I fucked up."

I lean forward and cup his jaw. "Hey, look at me."

His big brown eyes lift to meet mine.

"This is not your fault. Yes, we were both a little preoccupied with other thoughts and didn't think to call Sam. But those paparazzi were too pushy and not giving us any space. They are the ones who are at fault for this, not you."

"You got hurt with me—because of me."

I press my finger to his lips. "Enough. I will not hear another word about it."

He smirks before biting the tip of my finger. "I kind of like it when you're bossy."

I nudge his shoulder. "Then here's another order for you: Watch that video I sent you."

He shakes his head. "Not now. You're hurt and I don't want to——"

"Watch the video." I pout and clutch my knee. "Please, it'll make my knee feel better."

He arches a brow. "Is that so?"

I grin. "Yep."

He shakes his head but he takes out his phone and clicks on my text.

I rest my head on his shoulder as he turns his phone sideways and raises the volume, the video enlarging on his screen.

It starts with a woman answering her door in a silk robe. A muscular tattooed man steps inside and grips her by the neck, spinning her to press her against the wall. He pins her there, devouring her mouth in a sloppy, passionate kiss. With one hand around her throat, the other tugs on her belt and opens her robe, sliding his hand over her breasts. He pinches her nipple and she gasps.

Then he lifts her in his arms and fucks her against the wall.

Trenton's chest rises and falls as he watches. "Why this video?"

"Because it's fast and raw, like they're desperate for each other and can't get enough. Like he couldn't wait one more second to be inside her."

His throat bobs as he swallows. "And this is what you want?"

I nod, squeezing my thighs together.

He tosses his phone onto the cushion beside him and pushes to his feet. "All right then."

I watch him as he walks to my door. "Wait, where are you going?"

He swings open the door and steps out into the hallway. "I'll be out here waiting for you to take off all your clothes and put on a robe so I can fuck you against this wall."

He closes the door, and I don't even care that he slammed it because I spring off the couch and hobble into my bedroom, leaving the bag of corn to melt on my floor.

I leave my dress on the floor in my bedroom and replace it with a robe loosely tied around my waist. I stare at myself in the mirror as I fluff out my hair and take a deep breath.

Once we cross this boundary, there's no going back.

I know this, yet I can't seem to convince myself that we should stop. I *want* to cross this boundary, *want* to feel Trenton inside of me, and it goes far beyond wanting him to write a scene in a book, or wanting to erase the memory of Sheldon with another woman.

When I open the front door, Trenton's eyes bore into mine. Time stops, the world around us fading away. My heart pounds so hard, I can hear my pulse in my ears. It's a deafening rhythm that only beats this way when I'm around him.

Does he feel the same?

Trenton lunges forward and I gasp but it's cut off as he grabs me by the throat. He shoves my back against the door to close it and cages me in as he claims my mouth. His tongue parts my lips and surges inside, twisting around mine in a hungry kiss.

A warm trail of arousal trickles down my thigh at the feel of Trenton's massive hand around my neck. His free hand yanks open my robe and slips it off my shoulders before squeezing my breast. He tears his mouth away from mine as he licks a trail down my chest, and sucks my nipple into his mouth. His tongue swirls around the hardened bud before switching to the other one, and my back arches, pushing my tits in his face.

His fingers slide over my clit, and he lets out a loud groan. "Fuck, Cassidy. You're dripping."

He coats his fingers and then brings them up to his mouth, his eyes fixed on mine as he wraps his tongue around them, humming in approval. "Open your mouth."

My lips part as I stick out my tongue, and Trenton places two fingers inside. "Now suck."

With his other hand still clutching my throat, I suck his fingers into my mouth and work my tongue as if it's wrapped around his cock.

"I bet your pussy is throbbing for me, aching for me to fill you up." The hand around my throat squeezes harder as he brings his face close to mine. "Are you ready for me to fuck you?"

All I can do is nod and hum around the fingers in my mouth.

God yes, I'm so ready for this.

He releases me and digs into his pocket, pulling out his wallet. He fishes inside for a condom and tosses his wallet to the floor behind him. I unbutton his jeans and push them down over his ass, just enough to free him from his boxers, while he tears open the wrapper and slides the condom over his length.

He grips my hips and lifts me, pressing me against the door. I wrap my arms and legs around him, and he positions his head at my entrance. We're breathless, panting into each other's mouths, my hips rocking against his hardness.

He looks into my eyes and pauses, hesitating. I can see the question reflecting in his gaze, and I want to erase it until there isn't a speck of doubt left.

"Fuck me, Trent. I need you."

Then he plunges inside me.

I cry out as he fills me, stretching me wider than I've ever been before.

"Oh my god." He drops his forehead to mine and holds himself still. "Fuck, baby. You feel so good."

I grip his face and kiss him hard, needing to pour all of my emotion into him.

He pulls himself almost completely out of me before slamming back in, and he does it over and over again in a punishing rhythm.

My shoulders hit the door with each thrust, and his fingers grip my ass so hard it feels like they'll bruise my skin.

"You're mine, Cassidy." He grunts as he fucks me in deep, long strokes. "Mine. Do you understand me?"

"Yours. I'm yours."

He glances down between us, watching as he pulls out and drives back in. "Look how well you take me, like this pussy was made for me. Bouncing on my cock like it belongs to you."

I can't look away, so turned on by the way he moves in and out of me. I reach down and rub my clit, needing to chase the wave of mounting pleasure.

Trenton unravels as he gets closer, his words becoming more possessive.

"I want to be inside you every night."

"Fuck you forever."

"No one else gets to make you come like this."

"You belong to me now."

I want all of it—everything he's saying, everything he's promising. I know I shouldn't trust anything that's said in the middle of lust-filled sex, but my stupid hopeful heart latches onto his words.

I come hard, my body shuddering against him as I scream his name, and with one more thrust he comes with me. We're loud and unrestrained, and we're one.

Trenton's breaths are ragged as he presses a kiss to my forehead, then to the tip of my nose, then to each eyelid and cheek, before his soft lips meet mine.

"You're ruining me, Cassidy Quinn."

I smile at that. "Good."

Because you've already ruined me.

17

TRENTON

THE SUN STREAKS through the curtains hanging on Cassidy's window.

Her alarm clock reads 6:23AM.

It's too early for me to be awake after our late night, but I'm too wired to sleep.

I took Cassidy to bed after fucking her against the door like a savage animal, and she fell asleep within seconds of her head hitting the pillow. But me? My mind was reeling.

I'm in love with her. I don't know when it started, or how it happened, but I've been falling for a while now. Last night only solidified it.

I just don't know what she wants.

If I tell her how I feel, I could risk ruining everything. I couldn't care less about my image and this arrangement Celeste cooked up. But Cassidy needs to finish this book she's working on, and I don't want to take that away from her if I tell her how I feel and she doesn't feel the same.

I have to wait it out.

Cassidy turns over and buries her face in my chest. "Why is it so fucking bright in here?"

I chuckle. "Because we passed out without closing your curtains."

She sighs against me as I run my fingers down her bare back. "I don't want to wake up yet."

"So don't." I press a kiss to the top of her head. "We can stay here all day."

Her head pops up and she opens one eye. "Really? You don't have anything to do today?"

"Nope. The season starts on Monday so I get to rest a little before the madness starts."

"So why are you up?"

"Couldn't sleep. Thinking about last night."

Her body wriggles against me as she hums. "Last night was good."

"It was." I slide my palm over the curve of her ass. "You are an incredibly sexy woman."

She slips her hand between us and wraps it around my dick. "You want to recreate another video already?"

"Fuck the videos, Cass. Just fuck *me*."

I roll onto my back and take her with me, positioning her legs on either side of my waist so she's straddling me. The sunrays hit her like a spotlight, messy hair and full tits, her naked body like a work of art that I want to gaze up at for hours.

She rocks her hips against me, letting out a small moan. "I love it when you look at me like that."

"Like what?"

"Like you can't take your eyes off of me."

"How could I? Look at you." I pull her down on top of me and press my lips against hers. "You're perfection, Cassidy Quinn."

She shivers beneath me. "Do you think...could you maybe be on top of me this time?"

I shift Cassidy onto her back and prop myself up, hovering above her. "Like this?"

"Yes." Her legs wrap around my waist as she runs her nails along my back. "I want you nice and slow."

I know exactly what she wants, and my heart soars.

"You want me to make love to you, baby?"

She nods, her eyes bouncing between mine. "Is that okay?"

My chest aches, and the words almost slip from my mouth.

I love you.

Be with me.

I want to be yours.

Instead, I dip down and capture her lips. "I would love nothing more."

I show her everything I'm feeling, hoping she feels it too.

"Do you know how to care for them?"

I peer inside the cage. "I've been doing a lot of research. It seems fairly simple."

Ronaldo nods. "Just keep them away from direct sunlight and make sure the area isn't too drafty. She's cared for a bird before, you said?"

"Yes, she nursed a baby bird back to health after the nest fell out of the tree and the mother abandoned it."

"Great." Ronaldo beams. "Love birds are a true symbol of love and devotion. There is no greater romantic gesture than this."

My eyes flick between the two brightly-colored birds snuggling together on a perch. I've wanted to buy her a new bird ever since Candy died, but she needed time to grieve. During that time, I scoured the internet for the right kind of bird to keep as a pet. I found Ronaldo and we e-mailed back and forth for a few days until I made my decision.

Nerves bubble through my veins as I drive back home with the birds secured in the back seat of my truck.

I can't see Cassidy getting mad about this, but what if she isn't happy with the way I'm springing this on her? What if she isn't ready for another bird, let alone two? What if she reads into the meaning of love birds and calls me out on it?

I release a steady breath through my lips. No. I know Cassidy, and she's going to love this. A smile tugs at the corner of my mouth imagining the way her face is going to light up.

Rupert lets me borrow a luggage cart to make it easier to transport the birds in the elevator, and he shoots me a wink as the elevator door closes.

I send Cassidy a text when I get to her door.

ME: Can you open the door for be, babe?

"I'M STARVING. I really worked up an appetite with all that fucking we—" The words die on Cassidy's tongue when she opens the door and sees the giant bird cage before her.

She covers her mouth with her hands. "Oh my god. What is this?"

I pop my head out from behind the cage. "This is for you."

She inches closer to the cage. "There are two birds in there."

"They're love birds."

Her eyes fly to mine. "Who's are they?"

"Yours." I wipe my sweaty palms on my pants. "I bought them for you. I wasn't sure if you'd want another bird after Candy, but I know how much you enjoyed talking to her every day. And these guys have each other so they won't be lonely when you're gone." I slip my hands into my pockets. "I'm not trying to replace Candy, but I just...I want you to be happy."

Cassidy rushes into the hallway and wraps her arms around my midsection, squeezing me tight. "I am happy, Trent. Thank you so much. This is the most thoughtful gift anyone's ever given me."

I close my eyes and relish in the feel of her in my arms, relieved she isn't mad.

But while I hold her, her body begins to shake with quiet sobs.

"Hey, look at me." I lean back just enough to look into her eyes. "Why are you crying?"

She sniffles. "I have to tell you something."

"Okay." Unease creeps into my gut. "What's wrong?"

"Let's go inside."

Fuck me.

My stomach twists itself into knots as I carry the bird cage into Cassidy's apartment.

Here it comes. The talk. The *I know we've been growing closer lately but we're only doing this for the contract and we're nothing more than friends with benefits* talk.

I set the cage down against the wall and join Cassidy on the couch.

She clasps my hands. "We started off on the wrong foot when you moved here, but I've really been enjoying this time with you."

"So have I."

She chews her bottom lip, and then she blurts it all out. "I know I signed a contract, and I know we're supposed to be pretending to date, but somewhere along the line, this became real to me. I know it's my fault because I pushed us into fooling around, and that made things way more intimate between us. But we said we wouldn't lie to each other, and I can't keep pretending that I don't have feelings for you. And if you want to stop what we're doing because you don't feel the same, then I understand. I know it's a risk telling you this, but I couldn't keep it in anymore. Not after everything. Not after this." She gestures to the birds. "You're so good to me and I know it's all part of the contract but I just needed you to know, on the off-chance that maybe you do feel what I'm feeling."

My heart thrashes against my chest.

"Baby, come here." I pull her onto my lap and brush her hair away from her face, looking into her watery eyes. "The man who sold the birds to me told me that they represent love and devotion. Which is why I got them for you, because I wanted to show you how I feel about you—because I *needed* you to know. I'm in love with you, Cassidy. I've been falling for a while now and it's not because of the contract or the sex. It's because I couldn't *not* fall in love with you. You're beautiful and kind and caring and talented." I brush the tip of my nose against hers. "I love everything about you."

"Even my singing?"

"Even your God-awful singing."

A laugh bubbles out of her as another tear rolls down her cheek. "I love you too, Trent. I know you don't believe in *meant to be*, but I do believe that everything happened to us so that we could end up together, exactly where we are right now."

She loves me.

"Maybe we're destined to be together. Who knows? But I'd like to think that I'd choose you regardless of fate or some divine intervention. In any version of how this played out, I would've fallen in love with you because you're the woman of my dreams. You're the person I've been hoping to find. Everything feels right with you."

Cassidy smiles and rests her head on my shoulder. "I don't think I could've written a better ending to this story myself."

"Ending?" I stand with her in my arms and toss her over my shoulder as she squeals. "Baby, we're just getting started."

18

CASSIDY

THE NEXT TWO months are a blur.

The start of the hockey season swept Trenton into a whirlwind, and I've gone along for the ride.

When he's not on the ice, we're making love.

If he's traveling, I'm writing.

Our schedules are color-coded, thanks to Celeste, and packed with important events.

But none of it compares to the pressure of tonight's game.

Jersey City vs. Seattle.

Trenton faces his old team on their home turf, and to say that I'm nervous is an understatement. Trent says it's no big deal, but Celeste, Aarya, and I flew out in support nonetheless. And maybe it's not a big deal to him. Maybe he doesn't care about seeing his old teammates because he's happy in his new life, with his new team, and his new girlfriend. But I know how much he wants to prove to the world that he's not ready for retirement, and what better way than to stick it to the team who let him go?

The media has been dramatizing the rivalry between the ex-best friends. Journalists have rehashed every detail throughout the time-line of their friendship—regardless of whether they were facts or fabricated clickbait—to ramp up the conflict.

Several Seattle fans boo us as we take our seats, but I don't bother to look in their direction. I opted for floor seats behind Trenton's goal as opposed to the cushy box seats. I want to be as close to him as possible tonight. I need him to feel my presence when he's on the ice, and know that no matter what happens, I'm here for him.

"How did he sound when you talked to him earlier?" Celeste asks.

I hike a shoulder. "Fine. I think he just wants to get this game over with so everyone will shut up about it."

She nods. "We'll all be relieved when this is over. I just hope they win so we can give a big *fuck you* to Seattle."

"They'll win." I lean back against my seat and blow out a long breath. "I know they will."

The announcer crackles through the speakers as the spotlights dance around the stadium, and the crowd goes wild.

The Goldfinches skate onto the ice as they're introduced, and I jump up to cheer as Trenton skates around his net. I press my palm against the glass and he taps it with his glove before taking his spot at the crease.

The sound in the stadium amplifies as the announcer introduces each of Seattle's players. Adrenaline spikes in my veins as they skate in circles.

"That's him," Celeste shouts over the music, pointing to number seventeen. "David Petroski."

Aarya holds up her middle finger. "Boo! You suck, Petroski."

I snatch her hand and force it back down. "Dude, you're going to get us into a fight."

Celeste laughs beside me. "Trent will have to bail us out of jail after the game."

"That's the last thing we need." I shake my head. "Could you imagine the headlines?"

Aarya nudges me with her shoulder. "Would make for a great scene in your book though."

"I'm not looking for jail time, thank you."

When the puck drops, all conversation is lost. We're on the edge of our seats throughout the first period. Seattle is coming for blood, attempting shot after shot, but Trenton saves each one with ease. The period ends without any points on the scoreboard.

The game kicks up a notch in the second period. Players on both teams spend time in and out of the penalty box, and the checks are getting more aggressive. I cringe each time they're slammed against the plexiglass.

Finally, Krumkachova scores a goal. We cheer as loudly as we can, hoping the boys can hear us above the jeering crowd.

But that goal ignites a fire under Seattle.

Petroski flies across the ice, refusing to pass it to anyone. Stamos gets in his way to block him, but Petroski checks him so hard, he flies backward as if he stepped on a grenade.

Trenton hunkers down in position, bracing himself for whatever's coming.

Petroski takes the puck around the back of the net. His lips move, and I can't make out what he's saying, but judging by Trenton's menacing gaze as he whips around, I bet he can.

Petroski passes the puck but Krumkachova intercepts, and takes it back down the ice. When he gets close enough to take the shot, one of the Seattle defensemen rides him into the boards and he loses the puck.

It's a frenzy of sticks fighting to gain possession, but Petroski comes away with it once again.

"Fuck." I jump to my feet. "Somebody stop him!"

Petroski gets so close, he looks like he's playing chicken with Trenton. But he's not watching where he's going and he knocks into his own teammate who crashes into Trenton, sending the both of them crashing to the ice.

And then all hell breaks loose.

Seattle touched the goalie.

Both teams surround the goal, checking and shoving each other. Sticks and gloves slide across the ice as referees descend on the mosh pit, yanking players back to separate them.

Trenton gets up and rips off his helmet and gloves as he makes a beeline for Petroski. He shoves him back against the glass and pummels his face, landing shot after shot.

"Yes!" Aarya screams. "Beat his ass!"

One of the refs pulls Trenton off of Petroski, who's face is now covered in blood.

I breathe a sigh of relief as it seems like everyone is cooling down. But Petroski lifts his stick and slams it into Trenton's face.

Trenton's body goes limp in the referee's arms, and falls to the ice.

The crowd is silent, except for the sound of my scream.

Krumkachova and McKinley kneel down beside Trenton, talking in his ear, but he doesn't move. We wait for what feels like forever for the medics to bring out a stretcher. They roll him onto his back, and a pool of blood is left behind on the ice.

Aarya wraps her arms around me and Celeste holds my hand.

"Where are they taking him?" I ask, choking back a sob.

"The medical room." Celeste's thumbs move across her phone at lightning speed. "Let me find out what's going on."

Tears stream down my face as I sink into my seat.

"It's going to be okay, babe." Aarya smooths her palm over my back in small circles. "Deep breaths."

Worst-case scenarios flash through my mind as the game continues with the backup goalie in Trenton's place. I feel helpless, unable to go to him or be by his side.

"The medical staff is treating him now," Celeste says. "I'm friends with one of them, so she'll give us updates."

"I just want to know if he's okay."

"He's coherent and alert. Once they stop the bleeding over his eye, he should be able to get back in the game."

My eyes widen as I lean over to read the texts on her screen. "Back in the game?"

"He's not going to let Petroski take him out like that." Celeste squeezes my knee. "He's going to want to get back in there and finish the game."

I hate to admit it, but I get it. I understand what he needs to do.

I just wish I could hold him.

At the start of the third period, Trenton skates back onto the ice. Relief floods me as I jump to my feet.

He skates past the net and skids to a stop in front of the plexiglass separating us.

"I love you," he mouths.

I press both palms against the plastic. "I love you."

Trenton stops every attempted goal, and Krumkachova scores to secure a win by the end of the game.

2-1.

Eat shit, Petroski.

I PACE the perimeter of the hotel room until Trenton shows up after the game.

I all but throw myself into his arms.

He smooths his hand over my hair as he holds me against his chest. "It's okay, baby. I'm okay."

I sniffle as I lift my head and cradle his face. "Let me look at you. Show me what happened."

The skin around his eye is purple with a nice gash across his brow.

I gasp. "You shouldn't have played after that hit. You should've gone to the hospital."

He tugs my arm toward the bed and pulls me down onto the mattress with him. "Stop yelling at me and come snuggle me, woman."

I curl around his body and rest my head on his shoulder, listening to the sound of his steady heartbeat.

"I'm sorry I scared you tonight."

"It's not your fault. It's that asswipe Petroski's fault." My hands ball into fists. "I should've waited for him in the parking lot and backed my car into him."

Trenton chuckles. "So much violence inside such a small person."

"At least he got penalized for it. I hope getting tossed from the game and fined teaches him a lesson."

Trenton rests his chin on the top of my head. "I'm just glad we won."

"What was he saying to you? I saw his mouth moving but I couldn't hear anything."

"He said he's down to share my new girlfriend since I let him have the last one." His jaw works under his skin. "Said he could bend you over and show you a few things."

"Piece of shit." My nose scrunches in disgust. "He was just trying to get a reaction out of you. Next time someone makes a comment about me, don't fight them, okay? It's not worth it."

He lifts my chin. "You're worth everything."

19

CASSIDY

"I'm so happy to be back home."

Trenton leans down and presses a kiss to the top of my head as we enter our apartment building. "Me too."

When we step inside the lobby, Rupert greets us. "Great game, Mr. Ward. Sorry about your eye."

"Thanks, Rupert. Please, call me Trent."

Rupert nods and turns to me. "Hi, Miss Cassidy."

"Hey, Ru. Thank you so much for taking care of the birds for me."

"It was a pleasure. They're adorable."

"How are you?"

"I'm well, thanks." He glances over his shoulder. "Uh, you have some visitors."

"Visitors?" I look up at Trenton. "I'm not expecting anyone, are you?"

He shakes his head. "No."

Rupert clears his throat. "They said...they said they're your parents."

My stomach drops to the floor and my throat goes dry. "M-my parents?"

He nods. "I didn't want to send them up without your permission."

I peek around Rupert's tall frame, and bile climbs up my throat.

I've always thought my parents looked a lot like Matilda's in the movie adaptation: My father, a stout, greasy-haired man who always smelled like cheap cologne and cigars; my mother a much skinnier version of me, with bleached hair, sunken-in cheeks and way too much makeup on.

Unfortunately for me, I didn't have any super powers, or a teacher like Miss Honey to rescue me from the hell hole I grew up in.

"*Those* are your parents?" Trenton asks, looking at the same couple waiting by the front desk.

I grimace. "Ru, did they say what they wanted?"

He shakes his head. "No, I'm sorry."

"That's okay, thank you."

"Do you want me to have security escort them out?"

"No, I'll handle them." I flick my eyes to the paparazzi gathering outside the building, hoping for a picture of Trenton. "I don't want to make a scene."

Trenton slips his hand in mine. "You don't have to talk to them if you don't want to. I can have them escorted out and there won't be a scene."

I chew my bottom lip. "Why don't you go upstairs and I'll call you when I'm done with them?"

"Not a chance, babe." He squeezes my hand. "We're doing this together."

My heart swells and sinks at the same time, loving that he wants to stand by me but also not wanting him to bear witness to the mess that is my family.

"Say nothing. If you're going to stay with me, you can't utter a word to them."

Trenton's eyebrows press together. "Okay."

"Promise me, Trent."

"I promise."

I lead us over to my parents and school my features, not wanting them to see me sweat.

"Cassie, it's so good to see you, baby girl." My mother wraps her bony arms around my stiff body. "How are you?"

"Follow me." I guide my parents into the elevator, and press the number one instead of six when we step inside.

"Well, look at you." My mother drags her gaze up Trenton's body. "You're a big boy, aren't you?"

As soon as we start moving, I reach forward and pull the emergency button to stop us from ascending.

"What the hell?" my father shouts. "What are you doing?"

I cross my arms over my chest. "What do you want?"

He scoffs. "That's how to speak to your parents after six years?"

"Eight, but who's counting."

His top lip curls. "Still got that bitch mouth of yours I see."

Trenton's body goes rigid beside me.

I place my hand on his arm to calm him as I let out a sigh. "Look, we all know why you're here so why don't I save you the trouble: You're not getting a dime from me, so go back to whatever hole you crawled out of and leave me alone."

"That's so rude to assume we're only here for money." My mother reaches out to cup my face. "We miss our little girl."

I jerk away from her touch. "Cut the shit, Mom."

Her thin eyebrows dip down as her façade fades. "You're with a big-time hockey player now. You have plenty of money to spare."

And there it is.

I lean in, getting closer to her face. "I don't need hockey player money. I have my own money, and you'll never get a cent of it."

My father cackles a hoarse laugh. "You know, I figured you'd say that. Which is why I'm prepared to go to those paparazzi waiting outside and tell them what a selfish little cunt you are."

Trenton steps forward but I yank him back by his elbow. "Go for it, Dad. Have fun. I don't care what you tell them."

My mom purses her lips. "You can act as tough as you want, baby girl, but I'm your mother and I know you. You'd hate to have your reputation slandered all over town."

134

"You think you know me? You'd have to actually talk to me to know me." Emotion clogs my throat, and it only makes me angrier. "You can say whatever you want to say about me, but it doesn't matter. I stopped caring about what people think a long time ago, thanks to you. Run your mouth all over town, but you won't bully me into giving you anything."

"We just need a little something to get us through the holidays." My mother gives Trenton her best doe-eyed impression. "We don't have any money for food or warm clothes."

I grunt. "That's because you snorted it up your nose."

My father snarls. "You think you're so much better than us. But we're your blood. We know where you came from. So you can sit up in your ivory tower for now, but soon, it'll all come crashing down."

"You'd love to see that, wouldn't you? Some parents you are." I smack the emergency button and return us to the lobby. "You're going to walk out of this elevator when it stops, and you're going to disappear. I never want to see you back here again."

"You're going to regret this." My father grits his teeth. "This isn't over."

"Yes, it fucking is." Trenton grips him by the back of his neck and tosses him out of the elevator as soon as the door slides open. "Security will see you out."

My mother takes her time sauntering out of the elevator, giving me a sidelong glance. "See you again soon, baby girl."

I slump against the wall once the door shuts and it's just me and Trenton.

He pulls me against his body and wraps me in his arms.

Tears sting my eyes. "I'm so sorry you had to see that."

He pulls back just enough to gaze down at me. "Baby, you have nothing to be sorry about. I'm sorry that you had to grow up with parents like that."

"Thank you for keeping your promise. I don't want you to be involved in this. They'll go away eventually when they see they aren't getting any money from me."

The sudden publicity I've received dating a hockey star is like blood in the water to them. I'm surprised they haven't found me sooner.

Trenton takes my hand as we head down the hall, and he doesn't let go even after we've gone inside my apartment.

"Leave your bags. We'll unpack tomorrow." He tosses his duffle bag onto the floor. "Tonight, I just want to hold you."

I groan. "Please don't act all weird now that you've seen what a shitshow my parents are. I don't want your pity. I'm fine."

He brushes his thumb against my cheek. "It's not pity you're seeing when you look in my eyes."

I arch a brow. "Oh, no? What is it then?"

"It's the same thing I saw in your eyes last night when I took Petroski's stick to the face." He leans down and presses his lips to my forehead. "It's the kind of loyalty you feel when someone hurts the person you love. The kind where you'll do anything in your power to protect them." He brings his lips to mine. "It's loving someone so fiercely and hoping it's enough to glue together all the broken pieces of their past."

My bottom lip trembles. "I don't care about the past. It doesn't matter. All that matters is what we have right now. And right now, I have you."

I slide my hands underneath his shirt, my fingers moving over the hard ridges on his stomach, relishing in the smooth warmth of his skin.

"You do have me. All of me." His tongue sweeps across my lips. "And you're mine. Your heart, your mind, your soul." His hands skim down my back and rest over the swell of my ass as he grabs two handfuls. "Your body."

I arch into his touch, opening my mouth and wrapping my tongue around his. "Then fuck me like you own me."

Without hesitation, he picks me up and stalks into the bedroom.

At the foot of the bed, he tosses me onto the mattress. "Everything off. Now."

We scramble to tear off our clothes, and then our mouths find each other again.

I take Trenton's hand and bring it down between my legs, letting him feel how much I need him right now.

"Always so ready for me." He coats his fingers in my wetness, rubbing me and making my hips buck. "Turn around and bend over."

I do as he commands, getting onto all fours and resting my head on the mattress with my bottom in the air.

"This ass,"—a sharp smack pierces through the air as his palm connects with my bare skin—"is fucking perfection."

He kneels down behind me and drags his tongue all the way from my clit to my ass, circling around the tight hole and then repeating it over and over again until I'm a writhing mess.

But right before I break apart on his tongue, he pulls back. I whimper while he gets a condom from the nightstand drawer.

I feel him once he rolls on the condom, his tip teasing my pussy, sliding in and out in short gentle pulses.

"Please, Trent," I beg.

As soon as the words leave my lips, he slams into me. He grips my hips and drags himself out of me before plunging back inside. The sound of our skin slapping together in an unrelenting rhythm spurs me on. Then his hand wraps around my throat, while the other reaches around to play with my clit, and I lose all sense. He leans forward and grunts in my ear, whispering filthy things while he has his way with me.

And it hits me in this moment that I'd let Trenton do anything to me—any fantasy, have me any way he wants me—because I trust him.

I've given myself to him completely, and as scary as that is, it's the truth. He rebuilt the trust that someone else destroyed, and now it belongs to him.

I only hope he doesn't break it.

TRENTON

THE CAR ROLLS to a stop down a side street, and Sam makes eye-contact with me in the rearview mirror.

I turn over my wrist and glance at the time. "They should be here any minute."

My knee bounces while I wait.

When Cassidy's parents showed up the other night, it was a shock to my system. I'd heard about what shitty parents they were to her, but hearing a story pales in comparison to seeing it play out right in front of your eyes. I wanted to wrap my hands around her father's throat and squeeze until he turned twelve shades of purple.

Who speaks to his daughter that way?

Who speaks to my girl *that way?*

She is everything good and kind and gentle in this world, and I'm going to protect her any way I can—even if it means making a deal with the devil himself.

Five minutes pass and then Cassidy's parents appear at the side of our blacked-out Escalade. Sam unlocks the doors and they slide into the back row.

"I knew you'd come through," Allen says. The overbearing scent of his Old Spice tinges my nostrils.

I twist around in the seat and glare at him. "Make no mistake, I'm not doing this for you."

"You're doing it for love." Pam coos. "So romantic."

"A man in love is a dangerous thing." Allen winks at his wife. "He'll do just about anything for his woman."

"This is as far as my love goes," I lie. "You get what you want, and I get what I want. I never want to see you come anywhere near her again."

Allen clicks his tongue on the roof of his mouth. "That all depends on how much you're giving us."

I slip the check out of my coat pocket and pass it over the seat. "You'll be grateful for whatever I give you, and then you'll disappear from Cassidy's life."

Allen snatches it from my fingertips and shows it to his wife. "I think you left off a zero at the end of this number."

My jaw clenches. "I think I gave you too many zeroes."

He chokes out a laugh. "Are you saying there's a cap on your love for my daughter?"

I grip onto the door handle to keep myself from lunging over the seat and beating the piss out of this asshole. "Get out of the car. Now."

"You sure I can't persuade you to give us a little more?" Pam licks her lips. "I promise, I'm well-worth your time."

My stomach roils. "I said get out."

She pouts as her husband climbs out of the truck.

"Cassidy doesn't know you're here, does she?" Allen asks.

I don't bother responding.

He already knows the answer.

I wouldn't be here if she knew.

The second the door closes, Sam peels away from the curb. My head falls back against the headrest, and I rub my temples in small circles as unease twists my insides.

"You think that was the right thing to do?" Sam asks.

"I don't know, but I had to try something." I meet his concerned gaze in the mirror. "You saw them. I have to keep them away from her."

I'd give them all the money in the world if it ensures Cassidy's happiness.

Cassidy

"I can't believe your book releases next week."

Excitement bubbles in my stomach. "I can't believe I finished it."

Aarya slides off her coat and lays it across her lap. "Has Trent read it yet?"

"Not yet. I'm giving him a copy tonight after the game." My eyes narrow. "Wait a second—whose jersey are you wearing?"

Aarya shrugs like it's nothing. "I'm showing my support for Krum Cake."

My eyebrows jump. "Since when?"

"Since he stopped by my gallery last night and dropped off his jersey."

"Oh, he just *stopped by* to give you his jersey?"

She flips her hair over her shoulder and averts her eyes. "Yeah, he came by the gallery."

"Why would he come to your gallery to give you his jersey?"

"I don't know. Geez, what's with the Spanish Inquisition?"

I cough out an incredulous laugh. "Oh my god."

Her eyes dart to mine. "What?"

"You like him."

She scrunches her nose. "I don't like him. I barely know him."

"Says the woman wearing his jersey."

She lifts her chin. "It looks cute on me."

"And I'm sure it's going to be on his floor later."

She rolls her eyes. "It's just a jersey."

"It's never just a jersey." My thighs clench thinking about Trenton's reaction the first night he saw me in his jersey. "He gave it to you because he wants to see you with his name sprawled across your back."

Aarya pauses. "But he wants me to show my support for the team."

I shake my head. "Think about it, girl."

"Oh, hell no." She tears the jersey over her head and stuffs it into her purse. "I'm not someone's property. I don't need him to impart his insecure masculinity on me."

I shake my head as I chuckle. "He's going to expect you to be wearing it."

The lights go out and the spotlights circle the ice as the announcer booms over the speakers.

The boys skate out as they're introduced, and Krumkachova makes it a point to skate around to where we're sitting behind Trenton's net. He locks eyes with Aarya, realizing that she's not wearing his jersey, and he skids to a stop in front of us.

He smacks the plexiglass. "Put on your jersey."

Aarya crosses her legs and shakes her head. "No."

He grits his teeth. "Put it on."

She flashes him a devilish smile. "Make me."

His cheeks redden before he skates away.

I tilt my head back and laugh. "You pissed him off."

She grins. "Good. I like him when he's pissed."

Any woman would die to wear Krumkachova's jersey—one he personally delivered to her. Leave it to my best friend to not wear it on purpose.

We're halfway into the second period when my phone buzzes with a text from Celeste.

CELESTE: Have you seen this yet?

I CLICK on the link she included with the text, and my blood runs cold.

ME: What the hell is this?

Celeste: You didn't know?
Me: No, I didn't fucking know.
Me: Did you?
Celeste: No.
Celeste: God dammit, Trent. I'll clean this up.

"WHAT'S WRONG?" Aarya asks, leaning over my shoulder to see my phone.

I reopen the link and hand her my phone as emotions slam into me like turbulent waves.

Trenton met with my parents.

He met with them and didn't tell me.

Aarya scrolls as she reads the article. "Why was Trenton with your parents?"

"I don't know."

"This picture was taken today."

My gaze lifts to the ice. "I know."

"And he didn't tell you anything?"

I shake my head.

"Well, I'm sure he has a perfectly good reason for meeting with them."

"And for not telling me?"

She hikes a shoulder. "Maybe he's waiting until after the game."

If he saw them before the game, he should've told me then. Actually, he should've told me before he planned on meeting with them because then I could've told him not to meet with them at all.

What the hell was Trenton doing with my parents?

I look at Aarya. "Can we go home?"

"Of course." She grabs her purse without another word, and we leave in the middle of the game.

I'm quiet the whole way home, lost in my own head as questions assault my mind.

"Do you want me to come up with you?" she asks when the elevator stops at her floor.

I shake my head. "I need to be alone right now."

"I'm here if you need me. Call me tomorrow and let me know how it goes when you talk to him." She pulls me into a hug. "I'm sure there's a good reason he didn't tell you. He loves you, Cass. He's not Sheldon."

"I know," is all I can say.

Tears burn behind my eyelids but I don't let them fall. Not yet. I need to hear what Trenton has to say about the pictures of him meeting with my parents in a sketchy looking alley.

I already know what he's going to say, already know what he did, but I need to hear it from his mouth. I need him to look me in the eyes when he tells me the truth.

And I don't know what I'm going to say after that. It hurts too much to play it out in my head.

It hurts.

Trenton *hurt* me.

And that's something I never saw coming.

I take in a long breath when I hear the knock on my door, but all the air gets sucked out of my lungs when I see Trenton's handsome face on the other side of it.

I love him so much.

Why did he do this?

"Hey, baby." He drops his duffle on the floor. "I didn't see you at the end of the game. Did you leave early?"

I nod. "I wasn't feeling well."

Concern etches across his face. "What's wrong?"

I wrap my arms around my midsection. "I need to talk to you about something."

"Okay." He gestures to the couch. "Want to sit?"

I nod again.

My hands shake as I slip out my phone and take a seat beside him.

Trenton gives me a dubious look. "What's going on? You're scaring me."

I open to the webpage Celeste sent me earlier, and hold up the phone to face him. "This is all over social media."

His throat bobs as his eyes flick from the screen to me. "I can explain."

"Please do."

"I met with your parents today because I figured I could pay them off to stay away from you. You pretend like they don't affect you, but I know they do, and I wanted to take that pain away." He hikes a shoulder. "This was the only way I knew how to help."

Anger mounts in my chest like a wave. "But I told you that I didn't want to give them more money. I told you I went that route already, and they still came back asking for more."

"I gave them more money this time though." Trenton leans forward and clasps my hands. "Baby, your parents threatened you the other night when they showed up here. I couldn't sit by and risk something happening to you, especially not over money when I have plenty of it."

"They make idle threats because they're manipulating you to get what they want." I slip my hands out of his. "And you walked right into it. You showed them your cards. Now they know they can get to you, and fool you into giving them what they want."

"Well, I had to do something. I had to try. I don't want them to keep coming around and harassing you."

"Neither do I!" My voice raises as emotion swells in my throat. "But now they know you'll be willing to do anything to protect me, so they'll be back again. It'll never end. Nothing you give them will ever be enough because they're greedy pieces of shit who don't care about anybody but themselves."

My bottom lip trembles as a tear rolls down my cheek. "You promised me that you'd never lie to me. It was the only thing I asked of you when we started this. But today, you snuck around behind my back and did the one thing I didn't want you to do."

"I'm sorry, baby." He moves closer again to reach out and touch me. "I didn't mean to upset you. I didn't want you to know about it because I knew you'd tell me not to waste my money on them, but to me, it's not a waste of money. I'd give them anything they wanted if I could guarantee your safety."

"You can't guarantee anything, least of all when it comes to them." I push off the couch to stand. "I know you think you were just trying to help, but I didn't want you to do that. I didn't want them getting a fucking crumb from us. And you knew that. You knew how I felt, yet you totally disregarded my feelings. You didn't talk to me about it. We didn't have a conversation. We didn't make a decision together. You made a decision for me because you think you know what's best for me."

Trenton rises from the couch. "No. That's not what I was doing. I wasn't disregarding your feelings—I was thinking of your feelings and trying to help fix the situation."

"You went behind my back, Trent." I press my palm against my chest. "You went behind my back to the people I hate most in this world, you made a deal with them, and you didn't even have the decency to tell me. I had to find out on the internet. And if I never saw anything, would you have ever told me? Or would you have kept it from me like some dirty secret?"

He rakes his fingers through his hair, pulling at the roots, and I see the truth clear as day on his face. "I don't know. I just wanted to help you. That's all."

"I know," I whisper, my voice shaking as I speak. "I know you weren't doing it maliciously, but you can't ignore my wishes and do whatever you want. My feelings matter. My opinion matters. And I can't be with someone who doesn't hear me."

His face crumbles and his arms fall limp at his sides. "What are you saying?"

I swallow down a sob. "I'm saying I think we need to take a step back. We barely know each other and—"

"Barely know each other?" He walks into my space and cups my face. "I love you more than anything in this world, Cassidy. Don't tell me I don't know your heart."

Tears stream down my cheeks. "We moved really fast because of this whole fake dating thing, and I think right now I need to pump the brakes. I didn't expect you to do something like this to me, and it's throwing me for a loop. Maybe we don't know each other as well as we think we do."

He drops his forehead to mine, clutching my jaw. "Don't do this, baby. I'm sorry I went behind your back and gave your parents money. I'm sorry I hurt you. Please don't tell me I just ruined everything."

The desperation in his voice breaks me in half. How easy it would be to succumb to his plea and fall right back into how blissful our relationship was.

But bliss isn't always what it seems. And it'd be foolish to think this wouldn't happen again. If Trenton can go behind my back so easily now, what's to stop him in the future from doing something like this again?

I wrap my hands around his wrists and pull him from my face. "I just need some time. You hurt me, Trenton. I know you didn't mean to, but you did. And I can't handle knowing you went behind my back and lied to me. I just...I just need some time to think."

His dark eyes glisten with emotion. His mouth opens and closes but no sound comes out.

I take a few steps back and my heart wrenches in my chest as the distance between us widens.

His head hangs as he walks toward the door. He picks up his duffle on the way out, and he closes the door with a quiet *snick* behind him.

I almost wish he'd slammed it.

CASSIDY

THREE DAYS.

It's been three days without seeing or talking to Trenton, yet I don't feel any better. I thought taking time away would help me see things clearer, but all the time apart has done is splinter my heart into more pieces.

It doesn't help that each morning I find a single pink rose outside my apartment with a letter attached to it.

I unfold today's letter:

> *One more day until release day.*
> *I'm so proud of you.*
> *I love you.*

TEARS well for the second time this morning, but I blink them away.

Despite being mad at him, I yearn for him. I miss his touch, his lips, his intuitive eyes. I've had to stop myself from knocking on his door and flinging myself into his arms. Sure, what he did wasn't the worst thing a person can do. I understand his motive. I know he wasn't trying to hurt me.

Still, I can't shake the feeling of betrayal. Maybe it's because my parents were involved and it struck a nerve. Maybe it's because it triggered the feelings caused by Sheldon when he cheated. Regardless of the reason, I need more time to work through my emotions before I can talk to Trenton again.

I don't want to be with someone who's going to make decisions *for* me. I want a life where we make decisions *together*.

I walk over to the bird cage and stick my hand inside, scratching the back of Goldie's head.

Goldie and Finch, named after the Goldfinches.

It felt fitting to name them after Trenton's team since being traded is the reason we were brought together. Now, it's only a reminder of how much my life has been filled by him, and how empty it is without him.

"You're lucky you have each other," I tell them as they chirp back and forth. I close the door and lock it. "I'll see you later."

I throw my crossbody bag over my shoulder and head out the door. I woke up this morning needing clarity and guidance, so I visit the one person I know can give it to me.

Fifteen minutes later, I'm knocking on Sherry's door.

A wide smile breaks across Sherry's face when her eyes lift to mine. "Hiya, Birdie. What a lovely surprise."

I let out a breath of relief that she recognizes me today. "I missed you so I wanted to come hang out for a while." I lift the deck of cards in my hand. "Want to play Rummy?"

She claps as she rises from her recliner. "I haven't played that in forever."

I sit beside her at the small round table in her room and shuffle the cards before dealing them out. "How are you feeling?"

"I'm fine. How are you?"

She hums. "You want to try that again with more conviction?"

I chuckle. "Is it that obvious?"

"I saw it on your face the second you appeared in my doorway, sweetheart." She draws a card and discards another. "Where's Trent today?"

I chew my bottom lip. "I don't know. I haven't seen him in a few days."

"Ah. You had a fight."

I nod. "I don't know what to do."

Sherry sets down three Kings. "What did he do?"

"How do you know it was him?"

"Because if it was something you did, you'd know what to do to try to fix it."

Alzheimer's be damned, this woman is perceptive.

I tell her about what happened with my parents, reminding her about anything she may have forgotten about since we last talked about them years ago, and then I tell her what Trenton did.

Sherry heaves a sigh when I finish. "My grandson has always had a protective heart. He's made sure that I'm taken care of, and I love him for it."

"He loves you so much."

"His love knows no bounds." She reaches out to clasp my hand. "It's up to you to set those bounds. You've been fiercely independent your whole life. You've never needed anyone to take care of you. Having someone like Trent can be a lot to get used to."

"Are you saying I'm scared to let someone do things for me?"

Sherry hikes a shoulder. "Only you know how you feel, love."

I draw a card and set down my four-of-a-kind on the table. It's definitely scary to love someone, especially after being burned in the past.

"He's going to make mistakes. You both will. But I can guarantee you that after this, he won't make the same mistake twice." Sherry wags her index finger at me. "If Trenton knows he hurt you, it's eating him up inside and he's racking his brain for a way to make this right."

I whole-heartedly agree.

I know how much he must be hurting because I'm hurting too.

Sherry places her cards face-down on the table and leans forward. "My advice? Get mad. Yell at my grandson. Tell him how you feel and demand the things you want. You are a strong, capable woman, and you get to decide your own fate."

My throat thickens. "I really missed you, Sherry."

"I did too, Birdie."

I play four rounds of Rummy with Sherry before it's time for her to go to lunch. We say goodbye, and I take her advice with me as I head into the parking lot.

"Cassidy."

My head whips around at the familiar sound of Trenton's deep voice.

"Trent, hi." My heart races as I gaze up into his turbulent dark eyes.

"Hi." He slips his hands into his coat pockets. "How's Nana doing today?"

"She's great. We played Rummy."

"I'm sure she loved that." He reaches out like he's going to touch my arm, but he lets his hand fall before he does. "Thank you for coming to visit her."

I nod. "Of course."

We stand so close we can almost touch yet it feels like we're miles apart. My heart thrashes against my chest, begging to be released from the prison it's been in these last few days.

Sadness pools in his irises, purple crescents underlining his eyes the same way they do my own from tossing and turning all night alone in a bed that still smells like him.

"I, uh, I won't be able to make it to your game tonight." I fidget with the zipper on my jacket. "I'm having a release party in Manhattan. Aarya and Celeste put it together." I let out a laugh. "Pretty sure Celeste has made herself my unofficial PR agent now."

"That'll be great for you." He forces a smile. "Celeste loves organizing events like that."

"I know we're still under contract, so I can come to the next game if you want——"

"Stop." His voice breaks. "Don't reduce us to that."

Thick silence stretches between us, neither of us able to look away.

Come on, Cassidy. Say something.

"Well, have fun tonight." Trenton steps around me as he heads inside the nursing home.

And I leave feeling worse than I did when I got here.

"You look like someone took a shit on your birthday cake."

"I'm sorry. I'm just not in the mood for a party tonight." I rest my head on Aarya's shoulder. "But everything looks amazing. I'm so grateful for everything you and Celeste have done."

"I know it wasn't the best timing with everything going down with Trent, but we thought you could use a night out." Aarya hands me a champagne flute. "Have you decided which excerpt you're going to read tonight?"

I nod, my stomach churning at the reminder. "It's my favorite scene."

Despite how difficult it's going to be to read to a room full of strangers who think everything is blissful between me and Trenton at the moment, I think this passage is powerful and encompasses the whole message of the book.

Love conquers all. It's unconditional.

Before I left for the night, I wrapped Trenton's copy of the book and left it at his door. When he gets home from his game tonight, he can read it if he wants to. I left specific chapters and scenes flagged with notes, giving him a map to the innermost workings of my mind throughout the writing process. He's such a huge part of this story. He was my inspiration. And this book will forever be a piece of my heart because of him, regardless of how our real-life story ends.

I down the champagne and try to loosen up before taking my spot at the podium. The room is packed with close to one-hundred lucky winners who were chosen to attend this live reading. They applaud as I stride out in front of them and adjust the microphone.

"If you've been following me on social media for the last couple of months, you know how this book came about. A six-foot-two grumpy hockey player moved next door to me, and I decided to

151

write a book about him. This book isn't based on our actual relationship, but I poured so much of us into these characters that it
feels like I'm giving you a window into my own real-life love story.
It's personal and vulnerable, and I honestly think it's my best work
yet. So, I hope you enjoy it."

I flip open to the bookmarked page and begin reading:

*I STORM out of the room, grabbing my purse and shoving my feet into my
sandals.*

"Where are you going?"

*"I'm leaving." I spin around, glaring up at him as he follows me into the
living room. "And you're not going to follow me."*

*Garrett rakes his fingers through his hair. "Don't leave, Mia. Let's talk
about this."*

"What is there to talk about? This whole thing between us is fake, Garrett."

"It's not fake for me."

His words hang in the air between us.

My eyebrows push together. "What's that supposed to mean?"

*"It means that all this time we've been pretending to be in love, I've gone and
fallen in love for real. Every time I had to hold your hand, I wanted to hold it.
Every time you kissed me in front of people so they'd see, I'd been dying to feel
your lips. Everything I've done for you as your fake boyfriend has been because I
wanted to do it as your real one." He reaches out and grips my face. "I don't
want to fake it anymore, Mia. I'm done pretending I don't love you."*

My heart leaps into my throat. "What about the contract?"

*"Fuck the contract." He brushes his lips against mine. "Be with me because
you want to be, not because you signed a piece of paper that says you have to be
with me."*

*Tears threaten to brim over my lids. "But I need that money, Garrett. We
had a deal."*

*"I'll give you the money right now. You want it?" He digs into his back
pocket and pulls out his wallet before shoving it against my chest. "Take it. Take
all of it, I don't care. You can have anything you want, as long as I can have
you. Just tell me you feel the way I do."*

. . .

By the time I finish reading the scene, tears are rolling down my cheeks—as well as the cheeks of the women in the audience. They're crying for the same reason I am: The love the hero has for the heroine is beautiful, and true. It's a love everybody wishes to find in their lifetime.

I was lucky enough to find that love.

But finding it is only half the battle.

You have to fight to keep it.

And that's what I intend on doing.

Trenton

I pull out a tissue and blow my nose into it.

It's late and I should be asleep, especially after tonight's game—or last night's game, at this point. I've lost track of time reading Cassidy's book. It's like I can't read the pages fast enough, devouring every word she wrote as if it'll lead me to some magic clue about how I can fix things between us.

Seeing her at the nursing home was physically agonizing, having to stop myself from reaching out for her and pulling her close. And it looked like she wanted me to. I saw something in her eyes when she looked at me. Longing. Then, coming back to find her book waiting at my door for me...it was like she planted a seed of hope.

Maybe that's foolish to think.

Maybe she finished the book so this is her parting gift to me, and we're over.

But maybe she left it for a reason.

Maybe she's trying to tell me something.

Maybe I need to fight harder to get her back.

I close the book and set it down on my nightstand, reaching for my phone instead.

She thinks I didn't hear her, that I disregarded her feelings. Well, this time, I'm going to do it right. I'm going to help her. And she's going to be in charge of doing what's best for herself.

And maybe I'll get her back in the process.

22

CASSIDY

It's early when I get back to New Jersey.

Aarya had wanted to stay in Manhattan all day and do brunch, but I snuck out while she and Celeste were still asleep.

It's release day, and I just want to be home.

But my feet falter as I walk down the hall to my apartment. I blink to make sure I'm seeing what I'm seeing correctly.

A very large man is sitting propped against my door, his long legs stretched out in front of him, his head lolled to one side. A bright-orange bouquet of roses lays across his lap, and a cooler sits beside him on the floor.

My heart gallops in my chest, pulling me closer to him.

When I reach my door, I crouch down in front of him and take a moment to stare at his beautiful face. Dark lashes. Sharp jawline. Plump lips. I reach out and trace the new scar above his eyebrow ever so lightly.

His eyes slowly blink open. "Cassidy."

The sound of my name on his tongue mixed with the gravely tone of his voice wraps around my heart like a vice.

"Why are you sleeping in the hallway?"

He sits up and turns his head from side to side, wincing as he stretches his neck. "I wanted to be here to wish you a happy release day when you got back."

"What's with the cooler? How long did you plan on camping out here?"

He pops open the top and pulls out a carton of ice cream. "Mint chocolate chip to celebrate."

Tears threaten to spill over my lids.

This man.

"Come on, let's get you inside."

I unlock my door and once it closes behind us, I fling my overnight bag and bury my face in Trenton's chest. He drops the cooler and the flowers, and then his arms come down around me. But it isn't enough. I squeeze him tighter, needing him to feel everything I've been holding inside of me these last few days.

"Thank you for being here." My voice is muffled in his shirt. "Thank you for waiting for me to figure this out. Thank you for trying to help me—even though I'm mad at you, I still love you for it."

He pulls back and tilts my face up so he can look me in the eyes. "I'm so sorry I hurt you. I'm sorry I lied to you. I'm sorry I made you feel like I didn't care about your feelings."

"I don't want you to go behind my back. I want to do things together." I choke back a sob. "I just want us to be on the same team."

"You are my team, Cassidy." He thumbs away my fallen tears. "I love you so much. Please say you can forgive me."

I push up onto my toes and brush my lips against his. "I forgive you."

All the pain and doubt washes away with the surge of emotions that come flooding out with those three words.

"I forgive you. I love you. I need you," I whisper like a chant against his lips.

"It's been hell without you, Cass." He sucks my bottom lip into his mouth and bites down. "I've missed you so much."

I yank my arms out of my coat and let it fall at our feet. Trenton pulls my shirt over my head and reaches behind me to flick the clasp on my bra.

I moan at the feel of his massive hands cupping my breasts, arching my back as he sucks on my neck and makes his way down my chest. I slide my hand into the waistband of his sweatpants and wrap my fingers around his length as wetness pools between my legs.

He releases my nipple with a pop and tears off his shirt before pushing out of his pants while I finish undressing myself the rest of the way.

I reach for him again but he takes a step back. "Wait."

"What's wrong?"

He reaches down and digs inside the pocket of his sweatpants lying on the floor, pulling out an envelope. "I wanted to give you this."

I flip open the flap and pull out a familiar packet. "This is our contract."

"Rip it up, and we can start over." His Adam's apple bobs as he swallows. "I don't want us to be bound by some deal. I don't want you to make love to me because you need material for your next book. I don't want you to feel obligated to be with me. And I don't want you to think for one second that everything I do isn't for your happiness. I live and breathe for you, Cassidy."

I tear the contract clean in half and let the papers fall at our feet. I feel the magnitude of this moment. It's rolling off us in droves.

And I want to drown in it.

"I love you, Trent. I'm yours for as long as you want me."

"Forever."

He sweeps me into his arms and carries me into the bedroom. I bounce onto the mattress as he drops me, the comforter puffing up around me.

Trenton pumps himself in slow strokes at the foot of the bed. "Open your legs and let me look at you."

I let my knees fall apart, and it feels like he's touching me as his molten gaze skates over my bare skin. I lift my hips, letting him know I need him.

"God damn. So perfect." He kneels onto the bed and runs his knuckles over my clit. "Did you touch yourself while we were apart?"

I shake my head.

"Neither did I." He slips a finger inside me, and watches as he pumps in and out of me, a wild look in his obsidian eyes.

I moan and writhe beneath him, needing more.

He removes his finger and sucks it into his mouth. Then he straddles me and slides his cock over me, coating himself in my arousal. "I want to go slow with you, but I'm not going to last long. Not with you this swollen and wet for me."

"Fuck me," I let out on a breathless whimper. "I don't want you to go slow. I've missed you too much to wait another second."

As soon as the words leave my mouth, he reaches across the bed, yanks open the drawer in the nightstand to fish out a condom, and rolls it over his length.

Holding himself at the base, he slaps his cock against my pussy. "Knees up, baby."

I hike my knees to my chest and then he sinks inside of me, hard and fast. I see stars as he pulls all the way out and does it again, plunging into me as deep as he can go.

"I'm going to fuck you fast now, but make no mistake: I'm going to take my time with you later. You're going to spend the day coming on my cock. Do you understand me?"

"Yes. God, yes."

I lift my arms over my head, pressing my palms against the headboard for support. He tosses one of my legs over his shoulder, hitting a spot deeper than I've ever felt anyone before, and then he leans down and grips my wrists, pinning me to the mattress while he slams into me.

Trenton owns my body, ravaging me with wanton desperation. I'm at his mercy, and I let go, giving myself completely to him.

I come hard, and Trenton loses it as soon as he hears me, bellowing his release.

We're slick with sweat, gasping for air, and our cheeks are wet from our tears. It's sloppy and raw and wild, and it's exactly what we needed to come back together.

"I love you, Cassidy." Trenton lays on his side to face me and pulls me against him, pressing a kiss to the top of my head as he catches his breath. "You are the woman of my dreams."

"You're the man of mine." I smile. "We should make this a release day tradition—an all-day fucking marathon."

All of a sudden, Trenton jumps up and bolts out of the room.

I prop myself up on my elbows. "Where are you going?"

"To get the other part of our tradition."

A minute later, he comes back with two spoons and the gallon of mint chocolate chip.

"Look at you." He licks his lips as he takes me in, hair a mess, sprawled out on the mattress. "And I didn't even need tequila to get you to take your top off."

SOMETIME AFTER OUR fourth time having sex and a long afternoon nap, Trenton and I emerge from the bedroom for dinner.

Hamilton's, of course.

"I really loved your book, by the way."

My eyebrows hit my hair line. "You read the whole thing?"

"In one night. I couldn't put it down." He rests his pulled pork sandwich on his plate. "I loved the way it ended. I was hoping it meant you were coming back to me."

"I couldn't stay away for much longer." I reach out and clasp his hand. "I need you to know, I understand why you did what you did with my parents. I truly do. But I've been down that road with them before, so I already knew the way it would turn out."

"And I need you to know that I heard what you said about disregarding your feelings, and it won't happen again." He shifts in his chair to face me. "I actually came up with an idea that I want to talk to you about."

"An idea about what?"

"I don't want your parents bothering you ever again. I know you feel the same way, and I want you to feel like you're in control of the situation. So, I was thinking...maybe you should file a restraining order that prevents them from coming near you. If they violate that agreement, then they get jail time. It'll teach them to leave you alone, and it'll put it on record that they've been harassing you.

"I also think you should meet with my lawyer and write a will that states if and when you die, your parents won't get a single thing of yours. Make Aarya your beneficiary, or donate all of your money to charity. Whatever. But you need to start protecting your assets." He pauses. "Only if this is something you want to do."

My mind spins as I process everything Trenton said. "I think those are some great ideas."

"You do?"

I nod. "I don't want my parents to gain anything if something happens to me. I didn't even think about that."

"I don't *want* to think about that, but it's better to have these conversations than not, because often times, it's too late and then all the money left behind goes to the state."

"And I could change the will at any time, right? Like, if I get married and have children one day, I could change who the money goes to?"

Trenton arches a brow. "Only if the man you marry is me."

Butterflies explode in my stomach. "You think you'll want to marry me some day, Trenton Ward?"

"I know I do."

"And have children?"

"I'd put a baby in you so fast. You just say the word."

I cough out an incredulous laugh. "You're not kidding."

"Not one bit." He picks up his sandwich and mutters into it before taking a huge bite. "Let's just hope they don't get your horrible singing gene."

I kick him in the shin under the table.

TRENTON

Aarya glares at me from under her helmet. "I blame you for this."

I stifle a laugh. "But you're going to have so much fun."

"A trip to the ER does not constitute as fun."

"Ah, come on." Krumkachova throws his arm around her shoulders. "You're with me. I won't let you end up in the hospital."

Cassidy nods. "Trent didn't let me fall the first time we skated together."

"That wasn't on ice." Aarya gestures to her ice skates. "There weren't sharp, flesh-cutting blades attached to the bottom of your feet ready to—"

Her leg slides out from under her and her hands flail in the air as she slips, but Krumkachova is there to catch her. He wraps his arms around her waist, pulling her body flush against him to steady her.

"See, baby girl? I got you."

Her nose scrunches in disgust. "Don't call me baby girl. You sound like that creepy dude from the *365* movie."

Cassidy throws her head back and laughs.

Krumkachova glances at me. "Do you know what movie that is?"

I shake my head. "Not a clue."

Cassidy pats my shoulder. "We'll watch it tonight."

Aarya's eyebrows press together. "Isn't your reunion tonight?"

"I decided not to go." Cassidy hikes a shoulder. "I'm in such a different place now than I was when I received the invite. I have zero interest in going."

"Not even to show off your arm candy?" Aarya waves her arm in my direction. "It'd kill Sheldon to see you two together."

"I don't care what Sheldon thinks, or anyone else for that matter." Cassidy smiles up at me, and my chest expands. "I'd love nothing more than to sit home in our pajamas and watch Netflix instead of getting dressed up to hang around a bunch of people I can't stand."

"Good for you." Aarya squeezes her shoulder. "Fuck 'em all."

Cassidy's eyes drift to the entrance to the locker room. "Hey, who's that talking with Celeste?"

I crane my neck to see. "Oh, that's Stamos' wife, Kourtney."

Aarya grunts. "They look awful cozy."

Krumkachova and I whip our heads to her.

Aarya holds up her hands, feigning innocence. "What? It's true. Look at their body language."

Cassidy keeps her eyes on them. "Is Celeste into women?"

I hike a shoulder. "No clue. We work together. We don't talk about her personal life."

"You don't think something is going on between Kourtney and Celeste, do you?" Krumkachova asks to no one in particular.

I shake my head. "Stams mentioned they've been friends for a long time. They grew up together."

Cassidy hums like she's thinking, but she doesn't let us in on it.

"Not a bad deal if you're Stams."

Aarya smacks Krumkachova in the shoulder.

"Ow, what was that for?"

She rolls her eyes. "That's such a man thing to say."

"Come on. You're thinking it too."

While the two continue to bicker, Cassidy tugs on my sleeve. "Come on. Toby just walked in."

We closed the rink to host Toby's birthday party for his family and friends, and some of the guys on the Goldfinches agreed to give them some hockey lessons.

We spend the next hour with Toby and his friends, but my eyes are like magnets, following Cassidy wherever she goes. I watch her as she helps the boys skate; as she talks with Toby's mother; as she laughs with my teammates. My heart couldn't be fuller with the love I have for this woman.

She went from the nuisance next door to everything I never knew I needed.

Cassidy catches me staring and skates over to me beside the boards. "Whatcha lookin' at?"

"You." I snake my arm around her and pull her close. "You're getting pretty good at skating."

She winks. "I had a good teacher."

I lean down and press my lips to hers. "I love you. You know that, right?"

"I love you, Trent." She nips at my bottom lip. "And I can't wait to show you just how much later."

I hum against the crook of her neck, trailing light kisses along her skin. "I can't wait."

"Hey, lovebirds," McKinley yells from across the rink. "They're bringing out the cake. Quit sucking face and get over here."

I smile down at Cassidy. "Wanna race?"

She grins. "Game on, Neighbor Man."

THE END

Want to know what's going on with Celeste, Stamos, and his wife? Join my newsletter to stay up to date on what I have planned for my very first "why choose?" FFM romance coming out this fall!

Keep reading for a sneak peek of my emotional bestseller
Bring Me Back

New to me?
I always recommend starting with *Collision*
Book 1 in *The Collision Series*

Need something funny and light instead?
Check out my bestselling rom-com
Hating the Boss

Come stalk me:
Facebook
Instagram
TikTok

Want to be part of my warrior crew?
Join Kristen's Warriors
A group where we can discuss my books, books you're reading, &
where friends will remind you what a badass warrior you are.

All of my books are FREE on KU:

Collision (Book 1)

Avoidance (Book 2)
The Other Brother (Book3 – standalone)
Against the Odds (Book 4 – standalone)

Hating the Boss – RomCom standalone
Back to You – RomCom standalone

Inevitable – Contemporary standalone
What's Left of Me – Contemporary standalone
Someone You Love – Contemporary standalone
Bring Me Back – Contemporary standalone

Dear Santa – Holiday novella

ACKNOWLEDGMENTS

As always, so many people were a part of making this book come to life.

Dorthy, thank you for locking me in my classroom every morning before school so I had time to write this book (even if it was purely selfish so that I don't quit my job to become a full-time writer). I don't know what I would do without you. You are the best friend a girl could ask for.

Jason, thank you for all your hockey and goalie insight, and for lending me part of your personal story for this book. I appreciate you for letting me bombard you with questions.

Becca and Mary, thank you for always being my sounding boards while I'm in the middle of a writing process. I value your input and appreciate you more than you know.

Lastly, but most importantly: Stacy, thank you for letting me obsess over this book so I could write it as fast as possible. I know it's not easy being married to a writer but I appreciate all you do for me, our household, and for our family. I love you more than life.

BRING ME BACK

A Note from the Author

I have suffered from depression and anxiety since I was a child.

I know firsthand what it's like to feel helpless and alone, even with the most amazing support group surrounding you. I know what it's like to feel as if you can't trust your own thoughts. I know what it's like to constantly fight a war inside yourself. I know what it's like to be told you "shouldn't" be depressed. I know what it's like to feel like no one gets you. I know what it's like to feel less than everyone around you.

I almost took my own life when I was a teenager. I've been through some pretty dark times, but through it all, I held on to that faint ember of hope that things might get better one day. I'm lucky to be here to see that they can get better. My mission is to deliver that message to everyone who needs to hear it.

It's okay to not be okay, but it's not okay to not exist anymore.

If you're someone who is triggered by suicide, I encourage you to read this book. It might be a little difficult. It might make you cry. But I think you should push through. It's a beautiful story with an important message of hope, second chances, and learning to embrace who you are—scars and all.

"It's the Joshua tree's struggle that gives it its beauty."
—Jeannette Walls

1 | PHOENIX

Daily Affirmation: "I will stop worrying. I will learn to deal with my worries in a logical way."

I STARE up at the beige siding along the front of the house and blow out a heavy sigh.

It's kind of funny, seeking refuge in the one place I've avoided for so long. Life always seems to turn out this way. You waste so much time and energy steering yourself away from a particular path, yet you end up on that path regardless.

A deep-orange rust covers the three metal birds hanging above the garage. Dad loved those birds. I told him they looked tacky, but he insisted they stay. So, my brother Tyler and I named them and it became a running joke.

I tap out a text to Tyler: *Buffy, Willow, and Xander say hi. We wish you were here.*

I kill the engine and let my head fall back against the headrest. I don't know what I'm waiting for. I can't sit in my car all day—I have nowhere else to go, and it's twenty-six degrees outside. Besides, it's not like Dad is going to come out to greet me. His wide smile flashes in my mind, and my cheeks push up the slightest bit. It was impossible not to smile whenever he was around. He illuminated any room he walked into. I swear, the world got a bit darker when he passed.

Cancer can go fuck itself.

I close my eyes, count back from ten, and then swing open the car door. I hoist my bags out of the back seat, lug them up the driveway, and I don't stop moving until I'm twisting the key in the jiggly knob of the front door. Quick, like ripping off a Band-Aid, I step inside.

My eyes bounce around the entryway like a scared animal approaching a watering hole. Maybe if he didn't die here, I'd feel differently. Maybe we all would. My mother hasn't stepped foot in this house since his body was rolled out the front door, and my brother never looked back since he left after he graduated high school. I think that's why Dad left this shore house to me. He knew I'd need it one day. Somehow, he knew this could be my safe haven.

He was the only one who always knew what I needed.

Grief sinks into my stomach like a lead ball, splashing the bile around. For years, Mom hounded me to sell this place. *"You're throwing away your money. It's foolish."* But it wasn't foolish to me, and I'm glad I stuck to my guns on this one because it feels right being here after everything I've gone through. It's the only comforting thing I have left to hold on to.

I do a quick tour of the first floor. Eat-in kitchen where I used to watch Dad cook breakfast; living room with the brick fireplace we never lit because we only lived here during the summer; glass sliders that lead out onto the deck we'd jump off of every Fourth of July. Everything is exactly how I remember it, only now it's cold and empty. The vivid memories with Dad have been drained of their color.

Everything might look the same, but everything is different.

My combat boots echo off the wooden stairs as I head upstairs to my old bedroom, keeping my head down as I walk past my parents' room and focus on the thought of sleeping on a mattress bigger than a twin for the first time in almost two years. I drop my bags in the corner of the room and flop facedown onto the puffy white comforter.

My phone buzzes, and I scramble to get it out of my pocket. My heart sinks when Tyler's name isn't the one flashing across the screen, but only for a second. I clear my throat and try to mimic a cheery tone.

"Hey, Drew."

Drew's assertive voice blares through the speaker. "You're free. Why do you sound so sad?"

I roll over onto my back and stare up at the ceiling. "Being free isn't all it's cracked up to be."

"Sure, it is. Pizza, privacy, and porn, remember?"

"That was *your* list. Mine didn't include porn."

"Well, it should. Maybe that's why you're so damn depressed all the time."

I smirk. "What are you up to?"

"You know damn well what I'm doing: A whole lot of fucking nothing. The question is, what are *you* doing? How does it feel to be out of the looney bin?"

"Don't call it that." My eyes roam around my bare bedroom. "In a way, it feels like I never left. The world is the same, but there's more pressure now. Like I already fucked up once, so I need to do better this time."

"Dude, you're setting yourself up for failure if you think you aren't going to make any mistakes from here on out. You need to be more like me. Lower the bar. Expect to fuck up, and then when you do something right, you'll surprise yourself."

A slight smile curves my lips. "What am I going to do out here without you and your prolific advice?"

"You'll survive until I get out."

Drew has been my friend for the last sixteen months while I was at Clearview. I don't know how I would've survived that place without him. Not that it was so bad there; everyone was nice for the most part. But staying at a residential mental health facility isn't exactly the same as staying at an all-inclusive resort in Cabo.

"What am I going to do out here? What am I going to do with

the rest of my life? I don't have a plan." I slide my thumb along the scar on my left forearm. Some people bite their nails when they're anxious. Some tap their feet. I rub the physical reminder of the lowest moment in my life.

"Stop touching your scar. And don't tell me you're not, because I know you are." Drew clicks his tongue. "You're not supposed to focus on the past, remember? Look forward. Never back, always forward."

"Looking forward is what worries me. I have anxiety, remember?"

"You'll figure it out. You need to give yourself some time. You just got out this morning, for Christ's sake. You're not going to have all the answers on day one, so tell your anxiety to fuck right off."

If only it were that simple. I practice my deep breathing for a few seconds and try to slow my racing mind.

Focus on what you can control.

"What's on your to-do list? I know you made one."

I put Drew on speaker, and tap on my notes app. "I need to unpack, obviously, and I should stock up the fridge, so I'll need to go grocery shopping."

"Fuck that boring shit. Order a pizza and worry about substantial food tomorrow. You've been living on this organic free-range kumbaya chicken over here. Let yourself indulge on your first night out. Celebrate."

Celebrate what? The fact that I had to be deemed stable enough to live among normal people again? Or the fact that my mother disowned me because she took my suicide attempt as a personal attack against her? Or how about the fact that my schizophrenic friend who has limited phone privileges managed to check in on me before my own brother did?

Drew's voice cuts through my thoughts. "Hey, stay out of your head. You're going to be okay, Nix. It's just going to take some time to adjust."

"Thanks for calling." A pang of sadness pricks my heart. "I miss you already."

"Good, you better. I used my one call for you, which means I can't call the phone sex hotline later."

"Eww. Please don't tell me you actually do that."

"I wouldn't have to if you were game. Come on, Nix. Talk dirty to me."

I throw my head back and laugh. "Not a chance in hell."

"Prude. I'll call you tomorrow to check in. Have a slice of pizza for me."

As soon as I end the call, I search for a nearby pizzeria and order a large pie.

While I wait, I log onto Facebook. Clearview had a strict policy against social media, so it's been sixteen months since I've connected to the internet world. I used to be into scrolling through my feed. There's something oddly comforting in seeing that everyone else's lives turned out to be just as mediocre and meaningless as mine.

Notifications flood my account, all from people I haven't seen or spoken to since high school nearly ten years ago:

Nicole Paisley: You should've died.

    Roger Clementine: There's always next time.

    Jessica Armando: Selfish bitch.

    Billy Jenkins: Her poor family.

    Tarryn Desai: Loser couldn't even kill herself the right way.

    Jared Martino: The world would be better off without people like you.

Each comment pierces my heart like a bullet. I know I should stop reading them, but I can't bring myself to look away. These are people I grew up with. People I sat next to in history class. People I worked on science projects with. These aren't sad internet trolls living in dark basements with nothing better to do. They're regular people with jobs and spouses and children.

And *this* is the way regular people view depression and suicide.

I don't know why I'm shocked. I was raised by someone just like this. Humans tend to shun and judge whatever they don't understand. But that doesn't make it hurt any less.

"Insensitive assholes." I deactivate my account and delete the rest of my social media apps. I survived without it at Clearview, and the world really is more peaceful when you don't have instant access to everyone's thoughts and opinions.

Instead, I open the romance novel I'm in the middle of reading and try to convince myself that love isn't one big crock of shit.

Bang!

It's difficult enough falling asleep in a house by yourself when you have anxiety but being woken up by a loud noise only confirms your irrational fear that someone has in fact come to kill you.

I sit up, spine straight, and strain to listen. In Clearview, I learned all of the nighttime sounds, like the clanking of the vents whenever the heat was about to kick on, or the cries of the patients in need of sedatives, and the differing footsteps of the aides making their rounds. But I can't identify where this bang came from, or what caused it.

I have three choices:

I can call the police. But I don't know if I'm in danger yet, and it might be for nothing. I'd hate to wake the neighborhood with sirens and lights over a pan falling in the kitchen cabinet. Not a great way to make a first impression.

Choice Two: I can jump out the window to escape the possible intruder. But if I broke my ankle, I wouldn't be able to run away. Plus, the last thing I need is for someone to think I'm jumping off the roof to try to hurt myself again. I'll be back at Clearview in less than twenty-four hours.

My last choice is my least favorite: I can be a big girl and go downstairs to find out what the bang was.

After weighing my options, I grab Tyler's old baseball bat—the one I found in the closet earlier and propped against my nightstand in case I needed it for a moment like this—and tiptoe out of the bedroom.

It's fine. It's probably nothing.

Or it's an escaped convict here to murder you.

No, that's not helpful. Maybe a bird flew into the window.

Birds don't fly at night, you idiot.

Shit. That's actually true.

I peer over the railing at the top of the staircase, and moonlight spills onto the tile from the open door—the front door that was locked shut before I went up to bed. It's an intruder. It has to be. How else does the front door magically swing open in the middle of the night? My heart races. I need to get back to my bedroom so I can call the police. But before I can move, a dark figure appears at the bottom of the stairs.

"Hey!" His deep voice thunders, shaking me to my core.

My knees lock up, and I stand there frozen.

He bolts up the stairs, taking them two at a time to get to me.

Fuck, fuck, fuck!

I shriek.

I panic.

Then I throw the bat.

I legit throw the only weapon I have at the crazed killer.

Not the smartest move, but it ends up paying off. The bat cracks the man in the head and sends him tumbling back downstairs, buying me time to run and lock myself in my bedroom. I grab my phone off the nightstand and dial 911. The operator promises someone will be here soon, so I hide in the closet and pray the maniac doesn't kick down my door before the cops get here.

I'm not waiting long before I hear muffled voices. I creep across the room and press my ear against the door until a booming voice says, "Ma'am, this is the Beachwood Police. I'm entering your home."

That was quick.

I glance out the window, and my eyebrows press together. No police car with flashing lights. Not even an unmarked vehicle. The cul-de-sac is desolate at this hour.

It's not a cop. It's the murderer trying to trick me!

"Nice try," I yell through the door. "I know you're not the police. But you'd better get the hell out of here, because I called them and they're on their way."

"My name is Officer Russo." His footsteps are slow and heavy on the stairs, and his voice gets louder as he ascends. "I received a call about an intruder. I can show you my badge if you open the door."

"Where's your car?"

The hallway light flicks on, shining through the sliver of space under the door. "I live next door in the gray house to your right. Dispatch sent me to check it out before sending anyone else."

"Did you see the man downstairs who broke into my home? He needs to be arrested."

"Yes, ma'am. I saw him. You gave him a pretty nice bump on his head." His tone hints at amusement. "You said this is your home. Can I please see your ID?"

I snatch my purse off the floor and fish around for my wallet. "I'll slip it under the door."

After a moment of silence, he says, "Miss Bridges, the address listed on it does not match this one. Would you please explain why you think this is your house?"

Shit. "My name is on the mortgage, and the deed. But I just moved in today and haven't had a chance to change my license."

"Why don't you open up so we can talk?" Then he adds, "My badge won't fit under the door."

"Is the intruder in handcuffs?"

"No, Miss Bridges. He——"

"I'm not coming out until he's cuffed."

He chuckles under his breath. "All right."

A deep voice says, "You can't be fucking serious."

"You heard the lady. Place your hands behind your back." Metal clanks together, followed by Officer Russo's voice. "Okay, he's cuffed."

I crack open the door and peer into the hallway. An older man in uniform stands beside the younger intruder.

The man in handcuffs grunts. "This is ridiculous."

And that snaps my last thread of patience. "What's ridiculous is *you* breaking into *my* house and trying to attack me."

"I didn't attack you." He glares down at me. "You're the one who assaulted *me*."

"No, I defended myself after you started chasing after me." I gesture at the egg-sized mound on his forehead. "You got what you deserved."

The police officer frowns, and his forehead creases. "This place has been vacant since we moved next door. Figured it belonged to the bank."

The man in cuffs lowers his voice as if I'm not standing right in front of him. "How do we know the house is hers? Maybe she's lying."

I cross my arms over my chest. "I am not lying. I have the paperwork to prove it. And whether the house is mine or not doesn't justify the fact that you broke in, so you don't have a leg to stand on."

Officer Russo claps him on the shoulder. "She's got a point, kid. Care to explain what *you* were doing here?"

His jaw clenches. "Not now, Dad."

My head jerks back as my eyes bounce between them. "Dad?"

"I'm Jim Russo." He gestures to himself, and then to the asshole beside him. "And this is my son, James Russo."

I almost laugh. The cop's son is a criminal? "You're kidding."

"I'm sorry about my son's behavior. If you can believe it, he had good intentions when he came into your house tonight."

Good intentions for breaking into my house, and scaring the life out of me? I arch an eyebrow as my gaze roams over the cop's son.

He towers over me. With a square jaw and dark features, he bears a strong resemblance to his father—except for his thick brown hair, which is unfortunate for him because he won't be keeping much of it judging by his father's bare scalp. He's dressed in a white T-shirt with gray sweatpants—every woman's dream, if they're not also worn with the pair of handcuffs he's sporting—and he's as broad as his muscles are thick.

James Russo is one exceptionally good-looking criminal.

Figures.

"I think you owe her an explanation, James." Officer Russo's eyes soften with his voice as he addresses his son.

James drops his gaze to the floor and shifts his weight from one foot to the other in silence. "I was looking for my brother, and when I saw the light you left on in your kitchen, I thought…" He swallows before he pushes out the rest of the words. "I didn't expect you to be here."

"And there's supposed to be an apology in there somewhere," his father whispers loud enough for me to hear.

James's jaw tics before he sets his eyes on me. "I'm sorry for scaring you."

Damn. This guy barrels into someone's house in the middle of the night in search of his brother, and mine can't even shoot me a simple text to wish me luck on my first day out of a mental facility.

Curiosity urges my next question. "Why did you think your brother would be in *my* house?"

His father answers for him. "We haven't seen him in a while. Sometimes he squats here instead of coming home. He—"

"Can you uncuff me now?" James cuts in.

Officer Russo gives me an apologetic smile as he unlocks the handcuffs. Without another glance in my direction, James turns around and heads down the stairs.

Officer Russo pinches the bridge of his nose. "He gets upset when his brother disappears like this."

"He does this often?"

He shrugs like he doesn't know what else to say. "My boy will turn up when he wants to be found. Always does."

What does that mean? But it's not my business to keep prying into his family drama. "If there's anything I can do to help you find your son, please let me know. I watch a lot of *Cold Case Files.*"

Officer Russo chuckles. "That won't be necessary." He turns toward the staircase and pauses. "We're a sorry attempt at a welcoming committee, but welcome to the neighborhood, Miss Bridges. If you ever need anything, feel free to come by. Call me old-fashioned, but I don't like the idea of a young woman living here all by herself."

Warmth pools in my chest. "You don't have to worry about me, sir."

No one else does.

After he leaves, I close the door behind him and wedge a chair under the damaged knob in an attempt to secure the house.

That fucker broke my lock.

Keep reading HERE

Made in United States
North Haven, CT
11 October 2023

42639088R00104